TROUBLE IN TWILIGHT

Hot lead greeted Will Trent when he stepped onto Triangle land. There'd been a lynching, a price put on the head of the man who'd been his friend, and many were anxious to see rope stretched — particularly the elegant Myrna McBride and her hardcase Diamond M crew. They made it clear that Trent was not wanted in Twilight. But pushing him was the wrong thing to do, especially when another killing made the issue suddenly very personal.

*Books by Ray Nolan
in the Linford Western Library:*

HANG-ROPE AT HARMONY
SATAN'S SADDLEMATE

RAY NOLAN

TROUBLE IN TWILIGHT

Complete and Unabridged

LINFORD
Leicester

First published in Great Britain in 1993 by
Robert Hale Limited
London

First Linford Edition
published 2000
by arrangement with
Robert Hale Limited
London

British Library CIP Data

Nolan, Ray
Trouble in Twilight.—Large print ed.—
Linford western library
1. Western stories
2. Large type books
I. Title
823.9'14 [F]   08289395

ISBN 0–7089–5709–9

Published by
F. A. Thorpe (Publishing)
Anstey, Leicestershire

Set by Words & Graphics Ltd.
Anstey, Leicestershire
Printed and bound in Great Britain by
T. J. International Ltd., Padstow, Cornwall

This book is printed on acid-free paper

For
H. J. 'BASIE' VAN DYK
Compadre

1

A familiar chill traced a slow trail up Will Trent's spine as the gelding moved clear of the sparse pine grove and stepped on to the rim of the ranch yard.

Like the two smaller ones, the main corral was empty, the gate poles on the ground, looking as if they'd been dumped there in a hurry. Through the pine tops a late morning breeze sighed wistfully; somewhere a door or a loose board created a gentle clatter, and nowhere was there any sign of life or recent activity.

Skirting the corral, a rough wagon road travelled up a low hill, disappearing into denser timber, winding its way, he imagined, toward Twilight.

Trent walked the gelding across the open area, the feeling of apprehension now full born.

Off to the right, amid a bunch of

cottonwoods, hulked the barn, cook-shack, and bunkhouse, the latter big enough to accommodate eight men in a pinch. Its door stood slightly ajar, undisturbed by the breeze.

Of its own accord the horse stopped at the hitchrack in front of the house, its ears twitching. Trent twisted slightly around, his gaze raking the other buildings, sweeping the deserted yard, moving up along the wagon road into the timber.

Nothing. Yet the feeling of having eyes upon him persisted.

He turned his attention back to the house, to the ragged shards of glass gleaming in the front windows, the door hanging cockeyed in its frame. Warily he eased out of the saddle and climbed the three steps to the veranda. At the door he paused, momentarily, then shoved, scraped it open, and stepped into chaos.

Most of the furniture in the large room had been hand-hewn, both the essentials and those things a man might build in an effort to create a modicum of comfort in a place he could call home. Care and time had been invested in their creation: total disregard in the way they had been left.

Every chair lay on its back. Tables were overturned, the broad Indian rug scuffed up into untidy corrugations. The only thing still on its feet was a wide rawhide-covered couch, and that too appeared to be standing at the wrong angle. Ashes from the stone fireplace lay scattered across the floor; in the gray mess several items that had once adorned the mantel.

Beneath one of the windows, near to where five cartridge cases glinted dully amid glass fragments, a dark stain stretched across the floorboards and into the edge of the rug.

Trent heeled about and started out of the house, stopping at the door, eyes narrowing up at the pines and the road leading away from the ranch. He stood very still, watching, waiting. But if what had caught his attention had been a brief flash of movement, whoever, or whatever it was, had slipped back into concealment.

The gelding stirred uneasily when he came out on to the veranda. Right hand lingering near the holstered Colt, he began a slow turn toward the bunk-house, the sensation at the nape of his neck like the touch of ice.

At the same moment that he discovered the door now wide open, a rifle cracked from within the building, lead smashing into the wood behind his head. The gelding reared back, snorting wildly.

'Drop it!' a voice bellowed.

Trent hesitated, holding on to the gun that had found its way into his fist.

'Throw it down, or you're a dead man!'

Slowly Trent's fingers relaxed around the Peacemaker, letting it slip from his grasp to thud at his feet. A figure almost as wide and as high as the opening through which it emerged stepped into the sunlight.

'Get 'em up high!' he shouted, starting cautiously forward.

Trent allowed his hands to slowly rise. The man's face was round, burnt red and heavily freckled, his eyes spaced too close together. The hair showing from under the sweat-stained hat was the color of rust, the Winchester like a tightly gripped reed in his scarred hands.

'Who're you?' he demanded, halting at the base of the wooden steps.

'Could ask the same of you,' Trent returned.

'I asked a question, dammit!' The rifle jerked impatiently as if to punctuate his words. 'What're you doin' here?'

'Name's Trent. What I'm doing is looking for someone.'

'Baker?'

'This's Triangle; it's his spread, isn't it?'

'Won't be for long,' the other grinned. He rested a boot on the lowest step and killed the grin. 'What're you doin' here?'

'Thought we'd covered that ground?'

'Not by a long walk, we ain't.' He leaned forward, the faded green shirt and black vest straining mightily across meaty shoulders. 'Baker sent you, right?'

'Want to tell me what this is all about?' Trent asked, jerking his head at the house.

Red Face climbed on to the bottom step, reducing the distance between them.

'Same thing that's gonna happen to you, 'less I get some fast answers.' The rifle poked forward, almost nudging Trent's belt buckle. 'Where's that goddamned drygulcher holed up?'

Trent's mouth drew into a tight line. In their time he and Baker had been called many things, but that had never been one of them. 'Why would Baker be hiding?' As the question left his lips, from the corners of his eyes he caught another flash of movement up on the low hill.

Red Face noticed Trent's attention

suddenly diverted, and also turned. But only slightly, and he was quick to realize the mistake. But by then a boot was already lashing out in his direction. It caught the barrel of the rifle, lifting it high. Trent stepped in fast, tearing the gun from its owner's grasp, bringing it around to swing hard at his head.

Red Face tried to duck, but not fast enough to prevent the rifle stock from glancing off the side of his skull. Under the impact of the blow he missed his footing when he left the step, and went crashing on to his back.

Trent scooped up his own gun, dropped it into its holster, and pointed the carbine at the dazed hulk sprawled in the dust.

'Feel more inclined to tell me what the hell's going on around here?'

'You're dead, you son of a bitch!' The words hissed through clenched teeth. 'I'm gonna kill you with my bare hands!'

'That's assuming I ever let you get

7

back on your feet.' Trent came down from the veranda. 'Who are you?'

Button eyes glared back with an undisguised mixture of hate and fury.

The carbine tilted. 'Make me ask again and I might start remembering how close your shot came.'

'Wasn't aimin' to hit,' Red Face muttered, struggling to sit up. 'Wanted only to stop you 'fore you tried anything.' One of his big paws rubbed tenderly at the side of his broad skull.

'What are you called?'

'Mosley.' He retrieved his fallen hat and sloshed it back on his head. 'Ike Mosley.'

'Keep going. Let me hear what you're doing here — what happened to Baker.' Trent's eyes left Ike Mosley to cast a quick glance up at the rider who had come out from the cover of the trees and now sat looking down at the scene below.

'There's a thousand dollars on his head,' Mosley supplied with obvious reluctance.

Trent felt his forehead crease up. 'For what?'

'For killin' ol' McBride, that's what for.' Mosley spat into the dust, pressed his hands against the ground and began to lift his carcass. 'Don't make like you never knew there's a noose waitin' for him.'

'I didn't. And I don't recall saying it was safe for you to get up either.'

Ike Mosley dropped back on to his rump.

'You been staked out, hoping Baker would show?'

Mosley nodded glumly. 'Everyone figures he's hell and gone out of the county by now, but I got my own ideas.' He paused to stab Trent with another venomous glare. 'He sent you to fetch something, didn't he? Probably supplies. He's holed up somewhere, too scared to show himself.'

With one eye on the rider now moving slowly toward them, and feeling no need to explain his presence, Trent said, 'Get up and get the hell out of

9

here.' He tossed the Winchester into Mosley's lap.

Carefully climbing to his feet, Mosley took a better grip on the rifle, thick forefinger snaking through the trigger guard. The muzzle began to lift.

'Go ahead,' Trent said. 'It's as good an hour as any for dying.'

Whatever had been in the big man's mind was quickly submerged by other considerations. Tiny eyes held briefly on Trent, then, as if to signify his contempt, he spat again, wheeled about and lumbered off in the direction of the barn.

A minute later he reappeared, this time astride a big steel-gray, passing wide of Trent. Several yards off he jerked the animal's head over hard, forcing it into a tight turn. 'We're not through,' he bellowed.

Trent watched him moving off along the wagon road, touch his hat in curt greeting when he came abreast of the approaching rider, then suddenly dig spurs into the gray's flanks.

The rider entered the ranch yard, keeping the calico pony to a slow walk. From under a stiff black Stetson flowed hair that gleamed like molten gold.

She stopped half a dozen yards from where he stood, her face impassive, taking in the worn and faded brush jacket and levis, scuffed boots, gun hanging not too low against his right leg, the sun-bronzed face, and narrowed gray eyes that studied her and gave away nothing of what he might be thinking.

'Howdy.' Trent tipped back his hat, liking what he saw. She wore a fringed riding skirt and soft leather jacket, neither of which concealed the fact that underneath was the kind of figure that would cause heads to turn. An attractive green-eyed girl whose face was made for smiling, but which presently offered as much expression as the ground upon which they stood.

'Ike Mosley,' she said, 'isn't likely to forget what happened.'

'Friend of yours?'

11

'No,' she returned tightly. 'I simply happen to know who he is and what he's capable of.' Her left hand tightened the calico's reins as it tried to move closer to Trent. 'You've made yourself an enemy, Mister . . . ?'

'Trent,' he said, taking a few steps closer, frowning up at her. 'Been watching long?'

'Long enough.'

'Why?'

She ignored the question. 'What business do you have here?'

A girl, he judged, accustomed to speaking from a position of authority or power. 'No business. Looking for Baker, is all.'

A tiny grimace tugged at her mouth. 'I might have guessed. Another one after the money; same as all the rest of them.'

'First I heard about that,' Trent informed her, 'was from Mosley. Jeff's a friend.'

The girl's face remained void of expression. 'Do you know where he is?'

12

The question momentarily threw him. He shook his head. 'That what you were doing up there? Also waiting, hoping he might come back?'

Green eyes hardened a little. 'Of course not! I couldn't care less about Jeff Baker, nor what becomes of him.' The retort was firm, cold, and without much conviction. 'I was out riding. I — I saw you arrive, and — ' She shrugged, leaving the rest to float off on the breeze that tugged gently at her unbound hair.

'What happened here?' he asked.

She hesitated, her gaze shifting to the house. 'They raided the place . . . got two of Jeff's men.'

'They?'

Again she hesitated. 'Does it matter?' she asked, the question seemingly bitter on her lips. 'What's done is done.'

Trent kept silent, waiting for her to continue.

'They'd been stealing Diamond M stock.' She turned to face him again. 'Jeff and his crew. One of the men was

13

shot and killed. They, — ' her voice dropped to a shade above a whisper — 'hanged the other . . .'

'How about Baker?'

'Is any of this really news to you?' A slight sneer tinged her words.

'Every bit.'

The girl's shoulders sagged a little. 'He wasn't here when it happened. They're still looking for him.' Some of the hardness vanished from her eyes when they sought his. 'You really don't know where he is?'

Puzzled by the contradiction in her manner, Trent's head shook once again. 'Been some years since last I saw him.' He waited a moment, studying her face. 'Mosley called him a drygulcher . . . ?'

The lines around her mouth drew tauter. 'Which is why the reward was posted.' She sat suddenly upright. 'If you're really a friend of his, I wouldn't linger around too long.'

'I'll bear it in mind.'

'Do that,' she said.

'This McBride . . . he must've drawn

14

a lot of water to warrant a reward of that size . . . ?'

'Among other things' — she began turning the pony, speaking over her shoulder, her tone suddenly stiff and haughty — 'Rory McBride was one of the most important and respected men in the country.'

'Hold on,' he called as she started moving away.

She stopped, turning in the saddle.

'Be nice,' Trent said, 'if I knew who I'd been talking to.'

If it were possible, her face wore even less expression now. 'I'm Carol McBride,' she said, and gave him her back, urging the pony into a run.

15

2

His mind a tangle, Trent allowed the gelding to choose its own pace as they followed the road that would take them to Twilight.

Time and circumstance change many things. Especially men. If the charges levelled against Jeff Baker were true, what, he wondered, were the circumstances that had wrought the changes and put him under the shadow of a hanging rope?

Those things he'd been told did not tally with the man with whom he had once ridden. It had never been in his book to take anything that belonged to another. As for gunning anyone in the back . . . It would be a cool day in hell before he would swallow that one.

Yet time, he reminded himself, had changed Will Trent. Had not circumstances again sent him drifting hell and gone from Wyoming?

His thoughts turned to Carl Hindler, wondering how he was making out, if the money he'd been sent had yet arrived. Dammit, he ought not to have side-tracked, should not have elected to look up Baker. Carl needed him; there was work to be done, stock to be replaced, decisions to be made . . . He removed his hat, using his forearm to wipe the sweat from his forehead. Sure as hell a man's getting old when he starts taking a stick to himself. As the blonde girl had said, what's done is done. He was here now, and he'd not be heading home until he had found out exactly what was going on. Carl Hindler would carry on with the work; he'd do what needed doing; and the old man didn't need his help in decision making either.

The road moved through a high outcropping of rock, twisted and began to dip, descending into a narrow draw through which trickled a shallow flow of water. Across it was strung a corduroy bridge, presumably to make it easier for wagons using the route.

On the far side a tall ridge of rock poked up at the cloudless sky, reflecting the sun's rays in glorious hues of red and brown. Quickening its step, the gelding veered to the left, moving through low scrub, heading instinctively for the water.

'Anyone'd think you were thirsty,' Trent muttered, remembering the overturned water troughs at Triangle.

As the horse lowered its head and began to drink, Trent relaxed in the saddle and reached for his makings.

The Durham and papers were halfway out of his pocket when the first shot echoed from up along the ridge.

Thrusting itself away from the water, the gelding made the kind of sound it had never made before, its cry mingling with the quiet thunder of two more shots.

Trent kicked free of the stirrups and hit the dirt, the .45 already in his fist, eyes swiftly searching the rock

18

formation on the other side of the draw.

The horse continued to reel backward, dropped to its knees, then rolled flank-down, its cries stilled.

A violent curse ripped loose from Trent's throat as he scrambled for cover. The rifle echoed again, kicking up dust behind him. He fell face down behind a cluster of back-brush, twisting on to his side, right arm extended, the Colt scouting for the source of the gunfire.

Another shot tore through the brush and went a foot wide of its mark. But now Trent had some better idea of where his attacker was hidden. He fired twice at a V-shaped break in the ridge, aware that the range was too great for a beltgun. The hidden rifle barked back its response, the slugs creeping closer to their target.

Trent held back, the Colt lax in his fist as he inspected the terrain. To the west the earth swelled up in a rolling, boulder-littered slope that looked to be higher than the ridge, that would not

19

only afford better cover, but which would probably put him out of the hidden gunman's line of vision.

The problem was getting to it. At least thirty yards separated him from its lowest point, and even if he succeeded in reaching it the .45 would still be of no great use. On the other hand, he could not afford to stay where he was, tossing useless lead, waiting to be picked off.

He rolled when the rifle cracked again, kept going as two more chunks of lead slapped into the earth he had vacated. Then he was on his feet and running, rifle slugs snapping at his boot heels. He'd covered several yards when something tugged at his upper left arm. Abruptly he swerved, throwing himself to the ground, rolling to where the motionless gelding lay.

Up on the ridge the rifleman must have sensed what the man below was trying to achieve, for now he fired even more rapidly. But again the shots went wide of their target. Trent lay low behind the horse, waiting for the silence that would indicate his attacker was probably reloading. When it came, he lifted himself, snatched his own carbine from the scabbard, sprang to his feet, and went sprinting to the incline.

As he'd hoped, whoever was up on the ridge had lost his range. The silence that descended into the draw was like the pressure of water in his ears. Making use of the break, he began to move up the slope, seeking concealment behind the boulders and scrub.

Spaced seconds apart, from across the stream, came two more shots. Trent's eyes narrowed. He lined his sights on the crevice and let rip. The sound of lead twanging off rock face echoed sharply back to him. He lowered the Winchester, waiting. Seconds became minutes ... and the deathly silence continued.

He could feel the burning in his arm, the blood soaking into his shirt-sleeve, pasting the rough fabric to his skin. He gave the wound a cursory inspection,

21

then ignored it. There was only one thing he wanted now, and that was whoever hid up on the ridge.

A while longer he waited, then carefully began working his way farther up the rocky slope. He'd made but little progress when he stopped, listening. From beyond the ridge he could hear the sound of movement, of shod hoofs on stone.

He moved faster, scrambling up between the rocks, unmindful of what noise he made, until he was at a point that put him in line with the top of the ridge. From there he could see the land levelled out beyond it, the road reappearing from some concealed point, thinning off into the distance like a dusty ribbon, finally vanishing between low hills.

The noonday sun pressed hard against his back as he squinted down at the road, at the tiny swirls of dust hovering low above it. Ahead, bent low in the saddle, a rider was making distance.

Trent lowered the rifle, swore softly, and started down the slope, getting down on to his haunches when he reached his fallen mount. He laid a hand on its muzzle, stroking gently.

3

By the time he put the last rock in place, Trent's shirt was clinging to his back like a wet rag. Dragging his feet over to the shade offered by a few stunted pines, he flopped down beside his saddle, and uncapped the canteen. He took a short drink, rested back and rolled himself a cigarette, wondering what distance still separated him from the town.

He was still sitting there, contemplating the walk that lay before him, when gradually he became aware of the faint, distant crunching of wheels. He stood up and moved out of the shade to look back down the sunbaked road. From between a string of low hills rose a hazy cloud of dust. He built another smoke, and waited.

What seemed like a long while later a spring wagon appeared on the crest of the incline. Trent gathered up his belongings and stepped out on to the side of the road.

The wagon pulled up beside him. Holding the reins was a man somewhere in his late fifties; not too tall, slightly paunchy, and dressed in town clothes. He smiled down uncertainly.

'Looks as if you could use a ride.'

Trent tossed his gear on to the wagon and climbed up beside the driver. 'Much obliged.'

'Name's Thatcher. Charlie Thatcher.'

Trent accepted the hand that was offered. 'Will Trent.'

'Which outfit you with?'

'None. Just passing through.'

Thatcher got the wagon moving again. 'Picked a hell of a way to do it.' He rubbed hard at his left knee, face drawn into a tight grimace.

'Lost my horse,' Trent supplied.

Thatcher tossed a quick look back to where he'd picked up his passenger. 'You built that cairn?'

'Uh-huh.'

'For a horse?' Though he tried not to show it, the surprise was there in the older man's voice.

Trent shrugged. 'We shared a lot of good miles.'

'What happened? It take a spill?'

'Yeah,' Trent answered quietly. 'After it stopped lead.'

For the first time Thatcher noticed the dried blood on the upper part of his passenger's sweated shirt-sleeve.

'You — in some kind of trouble, son?'

'If I am, it's not of my making. Seems like someone took a disliking to me.'

'And — tried to kill you? That what you're saying?'

'Either that, or I got mistook for someone else.'

'Better let the law know about it,' Thatcher advised. 'After you get that arm seen to.'

It didn't warrant comment, as far as Trent was concerned, so he gave it none. For several miles they travelled in silence. Eventually Thatcher broke it.

'Reckon you must've come by way of

the McBride spread.'

Trent was a while in answering. 'No, Baker's. Only no one was home.'

Thatcher sighed heavily. 'Imagine not. That boy's in a load of trouble.'

'Way I heard it, Jeff's supposed to have bushwhacked one of the McBrides.'

'Old Rory himself.' This time the older man's sigh sounded almost regretful. 'Met up with him at a little park near Eagle Claw. Pumped two bullets in his back then tried to hide the body. Probably hoped — ' He broke off sharply. 'My mistake — or did you use the boy's first name?'

'Baker's a friend. Was my plan to look him up.'

'I'm sorry.'

Trent said nothing, lapsing into further thoughtful silence.

They topped another hill, from which the road began a fairly sharp descent, threading down to a small valley and a large cluster of buildings.

'Twilight,' Thatcher announced.

27

'Appreciate the ride,' Trent said. 'Would've been quite a walk.'

Thatcher hesitated. 'I take it you're not from these parts?'

'No; Wyoming.'

'Long way from home.'

It wasn't a question, so Trent didn't respond.

* * *

Though he'd not given it much thought, Trent had Twilight pegged for just another town, not unlike hundreds of others he'd known. But it was bigger, neater, better laid out, and even though shadows were already stretched darkly across the ground, there were still a lot of people about, horses tied to hitchracks, vehicles pulled up against the sidewalks.

They entered from the east, where a livery barn was sited at the start of the wide street. Thatcher stopped at it, rubbed his knee once again before carefully climbing to the ground. He

28

walked, Trent saw, with a pronounced limp.

Trent placed his saddle in the care of the owner, promising to be back the following day.

'Sheriff's deputy's named Miller,' Thatcher told him when they were back aboard the wagon. 'Want to go over and tell him what happened?'

Trent shook his head. 'Let it ride. Things like that have a habit of sorting themselves out.'

'Then let's get that arm seen to.'

In spite of Trent's protestations, Thatcher remained adamant. He halted the wagon in front of what looked like a small store with curtained windows. A sign dangling over the front door bore the legend: *Dr. Walter E. O'Conner. Consulting Rooms and Surgery.*

A small, bespectacled man, with a pot belly, and a fringe of pink hair poking up around ears a trifle too large for his head, O'Conner cleaned up Will Trent's arm, confirmed it was little more than a scratch, and slapped on

29

salve and a bandage.

'You'll live,' he said, turning to where Thatcher stood watching, leaving Trent to get back into his shirt. 'How's the leg behaving, Charlie?'

'Considering the lousy job you did of mending it,' Thatcher answered with mock sourness, 'it doesn't trouble me enough to consider coming back.'

'Should've taken the thing off,' O'Conner grunted. 'Would've saved us both a lot of bother. Man of your experience ought to know better than ride up a slope when there's blasting going on.'

Trent noticed Thatcher's face stiffen. He dug into his jeans, asked, 'What do I owe you?'

The doctor waved him away. 'Forget it. Next time he comes in bleating, I'll load this old curmudgeon's bill.'

For the second time Thatcher blocked Trent's protest. 'Save your money. The lousy sawbones has already made a fortune out of me.'

O'Conner grinned. 'And why not?

Since you quit ranching to become a part-time banker, you can afford it better than most people.'

With obvious dislike of the subject, Thatcher changed it. In a tone turned suddenly somber, he said, 'Trent here's a friend of young Baker.'

O'Conner squinted up at Trent. 'Wouldn't noise it around, were I you. Folks here are still steamed up over what happened to McBride.' He pushed his glasses higher on to his nose. 'Or does my advice come a little late?'

★　★　★

A tiny, dark-haired girl leaned into one of the two display windows of Jean Arden's Fashion Shop, flaring out the skirt of a pale lavender dress she'd just draped over a store dummy. As she backed out of the window her glance flicked casually across the street at three men talking on the sidewalk in front of O'Conner's surgery. She recognized

31

Charlie Thatcher and the medic, and immediately lost interest.

Almost back behind the counter, Jean Arden stopped, spun around and returned hurriedly to the window. But by then, saddlebags slung over his shoulder, bedroll under his arm the tallest of the trio, was moving away, and all she could see of him was his back.

* * *

Though it didn't quite match up to its name, the Grand Hotel was better than many others Trent had used. The lobby boasted carpets, tall potted plants, polished brass, and furniture which had probably been freighted in from San Francisco. The room allocated to him was small, but clean and comfortable, the walls adorned with a pair of faded Currier and Ives prints, and on the bed a feather mattress almost a foot thick.

Bathed and wearing a change of clothes, by the time he came downstairs darkness had settled over the town. He

32

looked into the dining-room, discovered it somewhat crowded, and went out on the street.

Most of the business establishments had closed their doors, but he found a cafe doing slow business, gave his order to the counterman, and took a table next to the window. He'd been in Twilight only a very short while, but already he'd seen several dodgers offering the $1,000.00 reward for the capture of Jeff Baker. In the cafe window was still another.

He drank the coffee the counterman brought over, wondering who had put up the money for the reward . . . the girl he'd encountered at Baker's place . . . and her particular interest in Jeff.

Leaving the cafe, he took a leisurely stroll up and down the boardwalks of the broad street, getting the feel of the town. His steps carried him past a small dress shop in which lights still glowed, but he gave it scant attention, moving on toward the strains of a tin-panny piano emanating from the next block.

If other places along the street had quit their trade for the day, the saloon's business appeared to be only getting started. He went up to the bar, bought a beer.

A couple of card games were in progress; two men clad in worn range clothes leaned against an upright piano, listening to the music, trying to peer down the dress of the plump redhead who tinkled the keys. But mostly those in The Avalon were there to drink. Including the red-faced man.

Trent turned back to the bar and reached for his drink, glancing across to where Ike Mosley leaned his bulk against the wood. For a long moment they locked stares, then Mosley dropped his gaze, quickly downed what was left of his drink, and headed for the batwings.

Next to Trent a voice chuckled softly. 'It would appear as if somehow you've quenched Mr Mosley's thirst.'

Trent moved his head and found the space on his left taken by a man almost

34

his own height, clean shaven and wearing the kind of suit that goes with either money or authority, or both. He shrugged.

'My name's Hugh Beaudine.' The dark-haired man's eyes performed a swift survey of Trent, pausing briefly on the tied-down holster.

Trent took the hand that was extended, found it soft and narrow, but the grip firm. He gave Beaudine his name.

'Your place?'

'Afraid not. That privilege belongs to Sam Quinn.' He paused. 'New in town?'

'Just arrived,' Trent told him, conscious of the man's eastern accent, the smooth, handsome features, the fact that he was wearing some kind of cologne.

'Looking for work?'

'No, don't plan on staying that long.'

'Well, if you change your mind there's always a job for a good man.'

Trent sipped his beer, not sure that

he cared for Beaudine's overly friendly manner, wishing he would find somewhere to go.

As if reading his thoughts, a card-player at one of the tables yelled, 'Hey, Beaudine — you coming in?'

Beaudine raised his glass. 'Naturally.' He smiled at Trent. 'Seems there are a few gentlemen anxious for me to have their money.' He deposited his empty glass on the bar, moved away, then stopped. 'Feel like joining us?'

'Thanks, not tonight.' Trent let him go, and went back to his beer, glad to be alone again.

In the mirror he studied the percentage girls who'd attached themselves to three middle-aged men, one of whom was short and fat, wearing a brown derby.

Then he caught his own reflection, and for a moment had the strange feeling that it was his father looking back at him.

His father . . .

A big man; a laughing and loving

man who, almost single-handedly had built the community's first church, who'd conducted the Sunday services because there was no other to do it. The kind of man to readily welcome three strangers into his home and to his table.

In return they left him sprawled in his own blood, his wife beside him. Trent remembered lying in the doorway, watching through misted eyes as they ransacked the house, feeling his own life slipping through the hole in his scrawny chest . . . a while later, stirring to the smell of smoke, the crackling of flames.

Those attracted by the smoke from the burning house, offered small odds on his survival, but he'd refused to die, and when finally they'd let him out of bed he was a different person. Still a boy of twelve, but now parentless, and alone, with something inside of him turned cold and leaden.

He'd waited only until he was well enough, then set out to satisfy the hate that gnawed at his gut like a snared wolf, hurting and furious to be free.

For two days he travelled, with no more than a little food tied up in a bandanna, with nothing to go on but the memory of the faces of the men, a vague idea of the direction they had taken, and recurring visions of the sightless eyes of his mother and father.

On the fifth day, footsore and hungry, he was picked up by a young sheriff's deputy and returned to the small Wyoming homestead and the people who had nursed him, given him a temporary home, who then set out to convince him of the futility of his quest. The law would find them, they said. And he'd believed them.

But they weren't. Not by the law, not by anyone.

He'd stayed, but he'd never forgotten.

He'd acquired an education, working to pay his way, wanting nothing for nothing, not even from the couple who had become his foster parents. He'd liked them, but never was he able to feel any real closeness. Just an old man

38

and woman to whom he was indebted. The cold thing inside of him seemed to have taken permanent root.

He finished his beer, signalled to the bartender for another.

The years, they pass quickly, he thought as memories of a war flitted through his mind. By the time it was over he held the rank of captain, with thoughts of making the cavalry his career. And he might have had he not been in a saloon, with time on his hands and nothing better to do than stand at the bar, watching a game of poker.

One of the players, a bearded individual who went by the name of Bull Gravatt, who sat with his back to Trent, was a bad loser. While holding what he must have believed to be a winning hand, he'd run out of cash. From around his neck he yanked a silver locket and flung it on to the table.

'That's worth at least twenty dollars, and don't none of you tell me it ain't.'

Nobody had.

Though he'd been watching, Trent's eyes were focused on something more than merely the game, and afterwards he would never be quite sure of what had really happened. All he later recalled was a voice raised loud in anger, a flurry of movement, a single shot, then Gravatt staggering from the table, collapsing slowly to the floor, dying but not yet dead.

Which was when, for the first time, he saw the man's face. Memories which had been clouded by time came flooding back in stark clarity.

He moved to the table where the sallow-faced man in the black frock coat stood, the twin-barrel derringer still in his hand.

'Mind?' He picked up the locket, his own hands trembling slightly as he opened it . . .

The years, they pass all too damned quickly, he thought, remembering that afternoon. The two tiny pictures which had been inside the locket were gone, but his mother's initials, engraved into the silver, remained for all the world to see.

When he left the saloon the locket was his. More importantly, realizing he was about to cash in, Gravatt had talked. Reluctantly, and with his last breath, but he'd talked.

Trent resigned his commission, but it took a while to free himself from the army and head for Oklahoma. From one town to another he went, asking the same questions, invariably receiving the same answers. But here and there he'd pick up bits of information, just enough to keep him going.

He'd worked at a variety of jobs since that day — cowhand, shotgun messenger, town marshal — never holding any for long. Each simply a means to an end, to earn enough money to continue the search.

It was in Dakota that an incident occurred, leading him into the profession which not only provided an opportunity for greater earnings, but which also permitted the freedom he needed.

Their names were Kobold and Franklin, the men he sought and, as he'd always known he would, he eventually found them. But their deaths failed to bring the satisfaction he believed he would feel. Instead there was only the empty realization of having reached the end of a trail, with nowhere else to go. And then inexplicable loneliness . . . a loneliness which, in spite of everything that had happened since, still persisted.

$\star$ $\star$ $\star$

While Trent leaned against the bar, Jean Arden waited at the door of Dr Walter O'Conner's surgery. Surprise registered on the little man's face when he saw who it was who had knocked. Hastily he bid her enter.

Once in his office, surprise changed to concern. 'Anything wrong, Miss Arden?'

42

Jean shook her head. 'No, I . . . I was simply wondering about something. I — I thought you might be able to help.'

'Be glad to,' O'Conner smiled. 'Sit down and I'll warm up the coffee.'

'No,' Jean said quickly. 'Please — don't bother.'

'No bother at all,' O'Conner told her, still smiling, grateful to have such attractive female company. 'I'd been looking forward to an excuse for another cup.'

'Doctor — '

O'Conner stopped on his way to the kitchen, looking back admiringly. Something about Jean Arden's fragile beauty never ceased to tug at his heart. It was an emotion he could not explain, not even to himself, but whenever he looked at her he experienced a quiet, disturbing sense of sadness. Perhaps, he thought, it was the memory of too many years too quickly gone, of lost opportunities, of a life that hadn't turned out anything like his youthful dreams.

'Yes . . . ?'

Jean hesitated, suddenly unsure of how to phrase the question. 'This afternoon — I saw you talking to Charlie Thatcher and — and someone else . . . '

The little medic frowned, pushed the glasses back on to the bridge of his nose. 'That's right. What about it?'

'The — other man . . . who is he?'

'Said his name was Trent,' O'Conner answered. 'Charlie Thatcher brought him in to get patched up.'

Jean rose slowly, straightening her skirt, trying to keep her hands from trembling, afraid O'Conner might hear the beat inside her chest. In another year she would be thirty, but her tiny figure was still that of a young girl, her breasts firm and full, her waist wasplike.

O'Conner squinted at her, concerned by the sudden pallor of her face. 'Do . . . you know him?'

She nodded, and sat down again, the

strength in her legs about to desert her. 'A — a long time ago.'

★　★　★

A loud, laughing shriek snapped him back to the present. He located the mirrored image of a girl with a heavily made-up face, saw her shove the derby-hatted runt back into his chair, and stalk off, her chin tilted high.

He reached for what was left of his beer, and something else in the mirror caught his attention. Through the batwings had come a tall, heavy-set man who walked with the hint of a stoop. A metal star gleamed against his leather vest.

Behind him traipsed Ike Mosley.

A hush descended upon the saloon as the pair cut a path between the tables. Trent turned to face them.

As they stopped before him, the man behind the star ran his left hand slowly over his thick gray moustache, eyes of the palest blue taking a quick

45

inventory of Trent, not missing a thing.

'This him?' he asked Ike Mosley.

'Yeah,' Mosley answered. 'That's the one I was tellin' you about.'

4

His name was Virgil Dunn, the man wearing the badge. The look he tossed at Ike Mosley was a long way from friendly. To Trent, he said, 'Believe you were out at Baker's spread.'

'There a law against it?'

'Depends. So how about you and me taking a trot over to my office where we can have ourselves a little talk?'

'Want me to take him for you?' Mosley was already unholstering his gun.

'Ike,' the marshal said, his eyes not leaving Trent, 'back off. Get yourself a drink and leave me attend to my business.'

Ike Mosley, though, wasn't yet ready to move.

'How about it?' Dunn asked Trent.

'You arresting me?'

'Acting somewhat hasty, aren't you,

Marshal?' Hugh Beaudine got up from the table at which he was sitting and moved to where Trent leaned his back against the bar. 'What's the man done?'

Dunn's face became suddenly stoney. 'This's none of your affair, Beaudine. Butt out.'

Beaudine's shoulders rose and fell in a small shrug. 'No, I imagine it isn't. But is this any way to treat someone who has just arrived in our town?' He smiled easily at the lawman. 'People might get the idea we're not quite civilized.'

'You suddenly become his lawyer?' Dunn snapped.

'Does he require one?' Beaudine turned to Trent. 'Do you?'

'Can't think why,' Trent answered.

'He was out at Baker's place!' blurted Mosley.

Beaudine lifted an eyebrow. 'And what does that prove?'

'He's probably got Baker hid out someplace, that's what!'

'Have you?' Beaudine asked, his tone

casual, treating Mosley's charge as something of no consequence.

'I told him once why I was there. Right now I can't think of a thing that would make me want to change any of it.'

'Quit wastin' time, Virg,' Mosley growled. 'He's one of Baker's thievin' crew. No two damn ways about it.'

Dunn made as if he hadn't heard. 'I'm told Charlie Thatcher brought you in. What happened to your horse?'

Trent's head moved slowly, stopping when his gaze fastened on Ike Mosley. 'Seems like some yellow-belly took a strong dislike to it. Hid himself and shot it out from under me.'

'Who the hell'd want to do a thing like that?' Dunn asked.

Trent shrugged, still looking at Mosley. 'Like I said; some snake, too scared to come out from under the rock.' The smallest smile twisted his mouth. 'Or maybe he was trying to get me, but his aim wasn't so good.'

'What the hell're you lookin' at me

for?' Mosley demanded. 'You tryin' to tell me somethin'?'

'No. Wouldn't think there'd be any need of that.'

Mosley pushed forward. 'You accusin' me of somethin'?'

'Well now,' — the excuse for a smile disappeared from Trent's mouth — 'far as I can recollect, nobody else knew I was up this way — and you were the only one I saw out at Triangle who was packing a rifle.'

A roar came choking up from Mosley's barrel-like chest, then a huge right fist was swinging. Trent ducked, slipped under the blow and came in behind. Mosley flew past, barely able to stop himself from crashing into the bar.

He spun around, this time his roar loud and furious, lips peeled back to expose crooked yellow teeth. Trent moved back as the other flung himself into another lunge, abruptly sidestepped, and as Mosley came within reaching distance, kicked his left foot out from under him. Glasses rattled on a nearby table when his heavy body hit the floor.

Shifting his position, Trent watched as the man began heaving himself up, waited until they were again facing each other, then brought up his fist from down low, smashing it into Mosley's wide jaw. The impact sent pain scrambling up his forearm. Mosley keeled back, twisted, and went down, his head striking the leg of a chair.

Virgil Dunn cast a swift glance at the circle of muttering bodies that had formed to watch, listening to the quick bets being waged, most of them favoring the larger Ike Mosley. He caught Beaudine's smile, the frowned question, but ignored it, making no move to intervene.

Mosley cursed violently as he struggled to push his bulk back on to his legs. He was halfway vertical when Trent stepped in to greet him. This time he spared his hands by crashing a knee into the red, distorted face, silencing the curses. Blood streaming from his

51

nose, Mosley rolled over on to his heels. Trent readied himself for another swing, but Dunn stepped in and caught hold of his shoulder.

'That's as far as it goes!'

Reluctantly, Trent let his arms drop to his sides.

Mosley, back on his feet, wiped at his face, saw the blood and let loose the cry of a crazed animal, hurling himself forward. Dunn moved quickly, shoving Trent aside, blocking the charge.

'Outa my way, Virg!' Mosley yelled. 'No son-of-a-bitch does this to me! *Get outa my way!*'

Without any hurry Dunn unlimbered his gun, poked the muzzle into Mosley's belly. 'Going to give me trouble, Ike?'

Mosley stood very still. He wiped again at his bloody face. 'You taking sides?'

Dunn smiled thinly. 'What I'm doing, Ike, is telling you to clear out. Now!'

Mosley hesitated, glaring at Trent. Then he wheeled about, snatched up his hat from where it had fallen, and shouldered a way through the circle of grinning onlookers.

'Ready to come with me now?' Dunn asked.

Trent tucked in his shirt, straightened his gunbelt. 'Why not?'

As he turned toward the batwings, he saw Beaudine smile, lift his hat an inch from his head.

$\star\ \star\ \star$

Dunn pushed aside a tray with an unfinished meal on it, and sat down, waving a hand at the chair on the other side of the desk. 'Thought you'd retired.'

Trent looked at him blankly.

'Fellow I used to know back in Utah was through here a few months back. We got to talking about old times, and your name kinda came up. Told me you'd gone ranching, or something. Which,' Dunn added, reaching into a shirt pocket for a thin cigar, 'is why I wanted you here so we could talk. Folks

53

get kind of jumpy knowing there's a bounty hunter in their town.'

Trent's mouth tightened; he'd heard that sort of thing before.

Dunn got the cigar burning, blew smoke at a lamp suspended over the desk. 'Okay, so most of the time you worked for the Palmer Detective Agency. Boils down to pretty much the same thing.'

Trent shrugged. Everyone's entitled to an opinion.'

'Going to tell me who you're looking for?'

'No reason not to: I already told everyone else who's asked. Jeff Baker.'

'You and the whole damn population.' Dunn made no attempt to conceal his contempt.

'Jeff's a friend.' Trent repeated what he'd told Thatcher. 'Few days ago I dropped off Russ Durand at the sheriff's office in Phoenix, then figured I'd spare the time to look up Jeff.'

The cigar came slowly out of Dunn's mouth. 'Russ Durand?'

Trent nodded. 'Alive.'

Dunn examined the burning tip of his smoke. 'That ought to have swelled your poke. Durand was carrying a good price.'

It brought no comment.

'So what's this story about ranching?'

'Got a place up in Wyoming,' Trent told him. 'Me and another fellow. Was doing all right until a blizzard near wiped us out. Taking the job to bring in Durand was the only way I knew of to get the money for fresh stock, make the repairs.' He took out his makings, slowly began to build a smoke. 'Lot of dodgers around town.'

'Also a hell of a lot of people anxious to see your friend stretch hemp.'

'Who put up the reward?'

'Myrna McBride,' Dunn answered. 'Rory's widow.'

The cigarette built, Trent found a match and scraped it against the sole of his boot. 'One thing I'm not clear on. When was Jeff supposed to have shot McBride? Before or after his

55

place was raided?'

'Two days after, and nearly three weeks ago.'

'Also heard one of Triangle's men was killed, another strung up. Who was responsible for that?'

Dunn rose, went over to the pot-bellied stove in the corner of the office, stoked it up, and moved the coffee pot over the plate. 'Not hard to guess is it?'

'McBride's crew?'

Dunn nodded, came back to the desk. ''Cept nobody'll say so. Anyway, it's out of my jurisdiction.'

'I get the impression,' Trent said, 'this McBride swung a big loop.'

Settling back in the wooden swivel chair, Dunn retrieved his cigar from a tin ashtray. 'A pretty damned big one.' His eyes had turned hard when he looked at Trent. 'Don't even think it. There never was a time I was under his orders.'

'Want to tell me about this Beaudine fellow, Marshal? He also got pull?'

Dunn pulled hard on the cigar,

exhaled harshly. 'That's another thing I can only guess at.'

Trent waited.

'Arrived here some eighteen months ago, set himself up a law office. Got in plenty tight with the McBrides — especially Miss Myrna, and pretty soon ol' Rory was mighty interested in expanding. Bought out several small spreads that sided his. Wanted Baker's place as well, but Jeff wasn't interested in selling.'

'What are you saying? Beaudine put ideas in his head?'

'Wouldn't have been hard to do either.' Without success, Dunn tried to keep the sneer out of his voice. 'Rory McBride always had himself figured as something extra special. He was as rich as any man needs to be, but if he was shown a way to become even more powerful . . . Well, who's to say?'

Trent frowned. 'What would be Beaudine's percentage? What would he gain by any of that?'

'Some day,' Dunn said, 'maybe

57

someone'll tell me.'

'There was a girl out at Jeff's place. Said her name was Carol McBride.'

'Rory's daughter,' Dunn supplied. 'What was she doing there?'

'Hoping to find Jeff, I think.'

'That don't seem likely,' Dunn muttered. 'Not after what happened to her father.'

'She also said Jeff had been rustling Diamond M cattle. That true?'

'Let's put it this way,' Dunn sighed. 'Some unbranded Diamond M stock was found on his place.'

'How'd anyone know that if they weren't marked?'

'They were. Small ear notches.'

'That the way McBride did things?'

'Not regularly, no. Story I was given is that they'd been suffering some losses, so they earmarked a bunch of heifers, then waited to see what happened.'

Trent killed his cigarette, stood up. 'How well do you know Baker?'

'As well as you can know any man, I

58

guess. Always seemed like a straight-shooter to me, but then — '

'He was,' Trent cut in. 'He wouldn't steal water if he was dying of thirst.'

The marshal levered himself out of the chair. 'That's what I'd like to believe, Trent. But him hiding out the way he is, it makes things look bad.' He deposited the cigar in the ashtray, hitched up his pants, and stroked his moustache, everything done to provide him with time to think, to frame his words. 'Plan on staying?'

'It was on my mind.'

'Then do Baker a favor. You . . . run into him, you'd be giving him good advice by telling him to give himself up. That way he'd at least get a fair trial, have a chance to defend himself.'

'Would he?'

Dunn's shoulders went back a little. 'If it's up to me. And that's the best chance he's got — short of being careful never to come back here.'

'And if he decides to do that, he loses everything. That how it stacks?'

59

'If he's not around to meet the mortgage payments and taxes, he'll lose it anyway. But that's not what I was saying. Lots of men would kill their mothers for a thousand bucks, you ought to know that.' Dunn's head shook, quickly. 'No offence. That didn't come out the way I wanted. What I meant was, the boy's options, they're pretty damned few.'

'You want me for anything else?' Trent asked.

'No, that's it.'

Trent moved to the door. 'Any objections to me moving on to Triangle?'

'Wouldn't matter if I did. I got no authority outside of town.' Then, he shrugged, a slow lifting and falling of rounded shoulders. 'Well, why the hell not? If Baker's a friend, he oughtn't to mind. Just one thing . . . Diamond M may not take too kindly to it.'

'That,' said Trent, 'will be their problem.'

'Now hold on a minute!' Dunn came

around the desk. 'You better not be fixing to start trouble.'

'Trouble's a commodity I never go looking for, Marshal.'

'Yeah? I saw what you did to Mosley — what you might've done hadn't I stopped you.' Dunn paused to scowl darkly. 'Not afraid to fight dirty, are you?'

'Not when the odds are against me.'

The scowl on the lawman's face gave way to a thin smile. 'Nobody's yet been able to take Mosley. If he'd connected, just once, you wouldn't have had a snowball's hope.'

'What I meant about odds,' Trent said. 'Besides, it was a good horse. Worth several Mosleys. I was attached to it.'

Virgil Dunn looked down at his boots, then back at Trent. 'You're sure it was him?'

'I'd offer good odds on it.'

'Then maybe I stopped you too soon. Maybe I should've just let you beat his head in.'

'Who is he, anyway?' Trent asked.

'Used to work for McBride. Don't know what he did, but it got him fired. Since then he's been loafing around town. Sometimes he'll — '

Footsteps came to a stop outside the office. Trent grabbed the door as it swung open, preventing it from slamming into his shoulder.

A young, round-faced man, wearing a neatly trimmed blond moustache and a deputy sheriff's star, stepped inside. He tossed a quick glance at Trent, a curt nod at the marshal, crossed to the stove and tested the heat of the coffee pot.

A shade sourly, Dunn said, 'Help yourself,' and came over to the door, motioning for Trent to move.

'About Beaudine . . . ' he said, when they were outside. 'You asked what might be in it for him.' He hesitated. 'How about McBride's daughter?'

Not sure why he was being told these things, Trent stood on the boardwalk, letting the suggestion sink in.

Sitting on the edge of the desk, the deputy could see the heads of the two men above the brass curtain rail. He watched as they talked, slowly sipped his coffee, positive that it had not been his imagination, that Dunn had been loath to continue the discussion within his hearing, and he wondered why.

Minutes later, when Dunn camc back inside and shut the door, the deputy was sitting in the chair Trent had occupied. 'Who was that?' he asked.

The marshal took his placc behind the desk. 'Name's Trent.'

The other nodded slowly. 'Heard he was in a scrap with Ike Mosley.' He tried more of the coffee. 'That why you had him in here?'

Dunn picked up his cigar, taking his time about relighting it, studying Dix Miller through puffs of blue smoke. What was it about the boy that lately irritated him so? The round baby face that seemed to wear a perpetual knowing smirk . . . the superior attitude he'd acquired in recent months? The discovery that Miller's appointment had been a family-political affair? Or was it maybe the stories that had come back to him, those involving Dix's talk about it being time for Virgil Dunn to surrender the badge to a younger man? Whichever, Dix Miller was no longer the friendly kid who had first ridden into Twilight to present his credentials.

'It's over,' Dunn said. 'Forget it. Mosley took a swing at him and wound up regretting it.'

Miller put down the thick cup, laced his fingers together behind his neck, and stretched out his legs. 'Friend of Baker's, right?'

'Where'd you get that from?'

The smiled response bordered on insolence. 'Bumped into Hugh Beaudine. Why?'

And suddenly Virgil Dunn realized what had eroded the trust between them: the company the boy kept, the people he was sucking up to.

'Getting kinda thick with him, aren't you, Dix?'

Dix Miller shrugged. 'Figure it pays to be on the right side of those who count.' He continued to smile across the desk. 'It don't bother you, does it, Virg?'

★ ★ ★

Leaning against the bar of The Border Queen, Ike Mosley's big hand tightened around the glass as he struggled to suppress his fury. Putting a bullet through the back of Trent's head would give him the most satisfaction, except that it was too risky. Too many had seen the fight; they'd figure out who'd done it. But there was another way to square things . . . maybe a better way. It all depended if they'd let him back on Diamond M . . .

While Mosley nursed his thoughts, Jean Arden was closing the door of her store, preparing to lock up for the day and walk the short distance to her boarding-house.

5

Except for the music and some noise from the saloons, the town had grown quiet, considerably cooler. Few people were out on the street, and those who were moved as if they had predetermined destinations.

The girl was struggling to lock the door of a small store when Trent saw her. He quickened his step, intending to offer help, but by the time he reached her she'd withdrawn the key and was turning, her face darkly shadowed under the shovel bonnet. He touched his hat, said, ''Evening,' and continued on in the direction of the livery barn.

'Hello, Will.' The greeting was soft, all but whispered.

Trent stopped, came around slowly, convinced his ears had played some kind of trick. Her head moved and the shadow slid from her face.

'Jean . . . ?'

'It's — been a long time.' Her voice was hesitant, a little husky.

'Jean . . . ?'

Jean Arden smiled. 'You're the very last person I ever expected to meet down here.'

Trent came in closer, a sudden tightness taking possession of his chest. He looked from the girl to the store window, remembered passing it earlier in the evening, and for the first time took notice of the name emblazoned upon the glass.

'This . . . yours?'

She nodded. 'And you? What brings you to Twilight?'

'Came to see a friend,' he said, anxious to get the explanation out of the way. He gave the window a quick, frowning glance. 'I don't think I understand . . . '

'It's a long story.' She opened her purse, dropped the key inside.

There were many things Trent wanted to say, but all he could manage

67

was, 'You — headed somewhere?'

'Home. It's been a long and tiring day.'

'I'll walk you.' Without waiting for consent, he took her elbow, releasing it as soon as she moved, saying nothing until they were mounting the steps to the planks of the next block. Then he stopped abruptly. 'The name on that window . . . it's your own . . . '

Jean looked up into his puzzled face, smiled ruefully. 'As I said, it's a long story.'

But not so long that it could not be told during the rest of the short walk.

Everyone regarded Dwayne Hammond as one of the most successful young businessmen in Kansas. In reality, the man was over his head in debt, a fact not revealed when proposing marriage to Jean Arden. Somehow he'd managed to hang on, keeping his problems secret for over a year, right up until the pressure became too much. Which was when he dipped into the small inheritance she'd received upon

68

her father's death. That, too, Hammond kept to himself. When eventually it was discovered, very little was left of her money. But by then the marriage was already riding a rocky road.

'We lost everything. The business, the house — everything.' She stopped at a gate in a low, whitewashed picket fence.

'You've . . . left him?'

'Will, I had no option.'

'I'm sorry.' Trent was only too aware of his own dishonesty.

She looked over her shoulder, at the lights glowing in the two-story house, then back at him. 'It's all right. Whatever there'd been between us had already been destroyed. Dwayne was drinking heavily; he — '

Trent raised a hand. 'Jean, you don't have to tell me any more.'

She conjured up a smile, as if to say none of it really mattered, but there was a sadness in the smile that said something different.

'After the divorce I had to find work. I moved to Boston, then to — ' She

69

broke off, shrugging. 'Anyway, here I am.'

As Trent looked into her face, saw the glimmer of moisture in the corners of her eyes, he had to still hands that ached to reach out and take her to him. He said, 'But you're doing Okay now?'

'Everything is fine,' she said. 'Just fine.'

Suddenly he had no idea what next to say. Jean saved him from further embarrassment. 'How about you, Will? What's happened to you?'

Briefly, he told her of the Wyoming spread, how he'd met up again with Carl Hindler, an old friend of his father, striking a partnership deal, and settling down. He left out the Dakota incident, the shoot-out that brought him to the attention of O'Hara of the Palmer Detective Agency, a meeting that turned him to hunting bounty while continuing the search for his parents' killers.

'I'm glad for you, Will. You deserve

70

it.' She unlatched the gate. 'Will you be in town for long?'

'Depends,' he said. 'Some business needs to be taken care of . . . then I'll be riding.'

They spoke a while longer, things of small consequence, and after she went into the house, he walked slowly away, thinking of a Kansas town called Bitter Creek, and all the things that might have been.

$\star \quad \star \quad \star$

At Brodie's General Store, the following morning, he purchased the supplies he believed would be needed at Triangle. On his way out he almost bumped into Charlie Thatcher coming through the door.

''Morning,' Thatcher flicked a look at the loaded gunny sack. 'Going somewhere?'

'Moving on to Triangle for a while.'

He continued on to the sidewalk, Thatcher trading a grin for a frown as

71

he followed. 'Hoping Baker might return?'

'Something like that.'

Thatcher stepped down to the hitching rail, standing to one side as Trent fastened the sack of supplies to the saddle of a glistening red sorrel.

'Been talking to Sud Engel. Told me he'd sold you a mount.' He studied the long-barrelled, deep-chested animal the way a man who appreciates good horseflesh might do. 'Didn't think he'd sell this one.'

'Didn't want to.' Trent finished with the sack, turned to smile at Thatcher who was again in a business suit, a gray silk vest smooth and tight across his protruding middle. 'Took some haggling and a lot more than I'd intended to pay.'

'Should've taken me along. I'd have showed you how to trim the old fox.'

Trent patted the sorrel's neck. 'I'm not beefing. He looks worth every cent of the price.'

'Take my word for it, he is.' Thatcher

removed his hat, ran a finger around the inside band, then fitted it back to his gray head. 'You think Baker will come back?'

Trent freed the reins from the rail. 'Right now I'm not thinking anything.'

'Well, I'd best get along.' Thatcher limped around him. 'You take care, son.' Already on the street, he stopped, wheeled around and came back. 'Forget my head if it wasn't fastened on!'

Trent waited until the old man was inside Brodie's establishment, then stepped into leather and turned eastward.

Nearing Jean Arden's store, he was tempted to stop and go inside. But he forced aside the impulse, said, 'Let's go, Red,' and allowed the horse to fall into a steady canter.

★　★　★

The first day out at Triangle was spent cleaning up, setting the furniture back the way he thought it was supposed to be, clearing out the glass fragments from the shattered windows, covering the openings with such material as could be found. When he was through he stood in the middle of the main room, hands on hips, nodding with satisfaction. Baker had every reason to be proud of what he'd built, and it was apparent he'd done so with an eye to the future. Trent wondered if somehow Carol McBride hadn't been part of those intentions.

He slept fitfully that night, waking to sounds that could only have been in his dreams — dreams that were regularly invaded by Jean Arden.

Before sunrise he was up, cooking breakfast, but again the dark-haired, blue-eyed girl occupied his thoughts. He sat in the kitchen, drinking coffee, remembering Bitter Creek, remembering Dwayne Hammond . . . He finished the coffee in a long swallow and went out to saddle the big red.

For hours he rode a wide circle, finding small knots of cattle wearing the

Triangle brand, a few strays feeding unconcerned. The grass was good and there was water, both in a stream that flowed leisurely between low hills, and in holes that looked as if they'd never learned how to dry up. It was the sort of spread Baker had often talked about owning when he and Trent had been in uniform, fighting in the same campaigns. It had sounded like a distant dream back then, but somehow he'd turned it into a reality, and now he had something worth holding on to. If he could.

It was mid-afternoon when he topped the hill which rose up behind the Triangle buildings. He dismounted, moved between massive boulders that blocked the view, and looked down on to the ranch yard.

There'd been a place much like it in Bitter Creek that he'd looked at long and hard, long before Carl Hindler had talked him into settling down. He might even have bought it had it not been for Dwayne Hammond.

He sat down on a rock, slowly building a smoke, remembering promises so easily broken.

Down below a shadow moved.

Trent stood up, dropping the cigarette to the ground, eyes narrowing down the long slope. The back of the buildings were to him and he could see nothing beyond, except the empty corrals. Again he wondered what had become of the horses. The shadow in front of the house shifted, grew longer, and then the figure of a man came into view. He walked halfway to the largest corral, paused to look up at the wagon road, then slowly retraced his steps and vanished from sight.

Trent put a boot on the discarded cigarette, ground it into the dirt. Sand sifted up, spewing forth two other butts. He got down on his haunches, picked them up, broke one in half. The tobacco was still fairly moist.

He dropped them, scooped back the dirt and returned to where, without relish, the horse cropped at tufts of yellowing grass.

There were two of them waiting for him when he rode into the ranch yard, standing in the heavy shadow of the veranda's overhang, rifles in their hands. Tied to the hitchrack were four horses.

The biggest of the pair shouted something which brought two others from the house. Trent couldn't see his face, but the voice belonged to Ike Mosley.

Without haste, he headed the sorrel for the nearest corral, dismounted and tied the reins to one of the posts. Slowly he crossed the open ground, stopping a few yards from where four pairs of eyes watched with amusement, wondering if he hadn't been stupid to ride in as he'd done.

'Waiting long?' The question went to a thin man with a very narrow face and dark sunken eyes, the tallest of the group. Everything about him, his stance, the way he was dressed, labelled him as the one who would be in charge.

'Get his gun, Ben,' he ordered, and a stocky man with a drooping moustache and a week's facial growth, started forward.

'Don't even try it.'

The one called Ben brought himself to a halt on the bottom step, looked back over his shoulder. 'How about it, Evan?'

The gaunt-faced man, parted thin lips in a humorless smile. 'He's not that stupid. He'd be cut down long before he cleared leather, and he knows it.'

Ben Keller hesitated. Something about the man before him, the calm gray eyes that held his, brought an odd quickening to his pulse. He took another cautious step forward.

'No further,' Trent snapped, and glanced up at the grinning countenance of the man whose outfit sported too much silver. 'You going to tell me what this is all about?'

As one, the trio came off the veranda; Mosley and the other man who'd been waiting outside, separating, moving wide of Trent, positioning themselves a few feet to his rear. The thin man stopped at Keller's side, his eyes slid over Trent, from boots to hat brim, and the smile became a sneer. 'Will Trent, huh?'

Trent was sure he'd never seen him before, but it was apparent the man knew who he was.

The grin was put back on the narrow face. ''Case no one's mentioned it, mine's Evan Lomax.' It was said as if it too was a name that ought to be recognized.

'Thinking of doing to me what you did to Baker's man?'

Lomax cocked his head, eyebrows raised in puzzlement. Up close now, his face resembled a thinly veiled skull, the skin stretched so tight. 'Don't know what you're talking about, friend. But we can accommodate any of your desires.'

Keller snickered, his confidence returned with Lomax beside him and Trent boxed in.

No one had to tell Trent that against four guns, that close, he stood no chance at all. 'I'm still waiting to hear what this is all about,' he said.

'Oh, hell now, didn't we tell you?' Lomax frowned again, this time in an expression of exaggerated apology. 'It's no necktie party, Trent. Just a friendly invitation from Diamond M, that's all.'

'And the guns? They here in case I declined?'

Lomax shrugged. 'Well now, you being a pal of Baker's, we weren't so sure we'd be received too kindly.' His thumbs found their way back to his belt and something in his face changed. For a moment Trent saw naked hatred staring back at him. 'Somebody wants to see you, and when she gives an order — '

A boot scraped close behind Trent. He started to wheel about, and never made it. Something hard and heavy crashed into the base of his skull. His legs gave way, and even before he reached the ground a boot was smashing into his ribs.

* * *

When Rory McBride had constructed the house he'd built for permanency. Borrowing much from the Mexicans, he'd blended in things perhaps remembered from a land far distant. In doing so he'd created something which, at first glance, seemed to have a regal-like quality, but a harder look revealed an inherent ugliness. The walls were at least two feet thick, the balcony travelling the full length of the upper floor enclosed by an ornate railing, every window equipped with heavy shutters.

It was dark when they rode through the wide gates of Diamond M, up to the white monster that was a cross between a small castle and a fort. Trent had long ago regained consciousness, finding himself astride his saddle, hands lashed tightly to the horn, the horse

81

being led by one of Lomax's men.

They stopped at the main entrance, tied the horses to the rail.

'Cut him loose,' Lomax ordered, and Ben Keller produced a knife and slashed quickly at the bonds.

'Sorry it had to be this way, Mr Trent, but Mosley got a bit impatient with proceedings.' Evan Lomax's thin face split into a smile, but again hostility put a dull glint into his eyes. 'No hard feelings.' He nodded toward the house. 'Shall we go?'

Trent shook off the hands that tried to grab his arms and shove him forward. He followed Lomax, the others trailed close at his heels.

Lomax led the way to a wide, brightly lit and lavishly furnished room. Trent remembered what Virgil Dunn had said about McBride being as rich as any man needed to be. If so, it was obvious he'd wanted to prove it.

Or perhaps, he thought, that had been the idea of the woman who sat at the end of the long polished table.

'This's him, ma'am,' Lomax said, and stood aside so there was nothing between her and Trent.

She nodded, rose slowly, elegantly to her feet. 'I am Myrna McBride, Mr Trent. Thank you for coming.'

Trent almost laughed. But he didn't. Whatever he'd been expecting of McBride's widow, the woman in the high-collared black dress was not it.

6

Her dark auburn hair was tied back in a matronly chignon, touched at the temples by silver. Trent figured her to be in her late forties, but he couldn't be sure, for time had treated both her face and body with extreme kindness. A strikingly good-looking woman who spoke and moved with genteel grace. He could see something of her daughter in her, but not much.

A little to her left stood a stocky man with a long, square face and heavy brows. For a long moment he studied Trent, then gave his attention to Evan Lomax.

'All right; you can go now. Take the others with you.'

'You sure that's what you want, Jesse?' Thin lips slid back in a ghost of a smile. 'You got any idea who this jasper is?' Without waiting for a reply, he said, 'A stinking bounty hunter, that's what.'

Myrna McBride's head came up a fraction, but her expression remained impassive.

'I said you can go.' A hardness in the stocky man's tone wiped the smile from Lomax's narrow face and brought a quick narrowing to his eyes.

He jerked Trent's gun free from where he'd tucked it behind his belt, and slid it across the table. 'Then you better keep this.'

'Jesse,' Ike Mosley piped, 'give me a few minutes alone with him and he'll tell you where to find Baker. I guarantee it.'

'You were asked to leave.' Myrna McBride had no need to raise her voice to take charge.

He may not have liked it, but without a word, Lomax nodded to the others, and they trailed out after him.

When they were alone, Myrna McBride said, 'This gentleman is Jesse Finch, my foreman.' She indicated a chair. 'Please take a seat.'

'Thanks,' Trent said, 'but after being clubbed with the butt of a Winchester and brought here like a prisoner, I think I'd prefer to stand.'

'Those were not my orders, Mr Trent, and you're certainly not a prisoner.'

'No? Then tell me why I'm here.'

'First, perhaps you'll tell me what you're doing on Triangle?'

'How about if I said that comes under the heading of my business?'

'Watch your mouth!' Jesse Finch snapped, picking up Trent's gun from the table, coming around to stand beside his employer.

For several seconds silence reigned. Then Myrna McBride said, 'Return his gun, Jesse.'

Finch transferred the Peacemaker to his left hand, held it out butt-first to Trent, his free hand staying close to his own holstered gun.

Trent took it, slid it back between leather.

86

'Does that convince you?' the woman asked.

Trent's head still ached, but he tried to ignore it. 'No, but I'm in a better mood to listen to your reason for having me hauled here.'

'It's true? You're a — bounty hunter?'

'Among other things.'

For the briefest second indecision clouded her green eyes. 'The reward I've offered — is that why you're at Baker's ranch?'

Trent smiled. 'Uh-huh, but not for the reason you're thinking. Jeff's a friend.'

'He's a goddamn backshooter!' Finch retorted.

'Of that,' said Trent, 'I'd need a whole lot of convincing.'

Myrna McBride sank back into the heavy high-backed chair, slim white hands clasped together on the table's polished surface. 'Jeff Baker,' she said tightly, 'cold-bloodedly murdered my husband, Mr Trent.'

'Left him lying in the rocks near

87

Eagle Claw,' Finch added, making it sound as if he needed to spit. 'If a couple of our riders hadn't gone to see why there were buzzards — '

'Please, Jesse,' the woman said, 'I'd rather not be reminded of that day.' Green eyes switched back to Trent and her voice turned to ice. 'Now I'll tell you why I wanted to see you,' she said.

'Because you think I know where Baker is, and you want him. That it?'

'Do you know?'

'If I did, I wouldn't be telling anyone.'

'Does a man in your — profession,' she asked, hesitating over the word, 'need to be told the consequences of aiding and abetting a fugitive?'

'No, but he'd probably want proof of the charges against the man, and so far I haven't heard any. Not from anyone.'

'Baker was rustling our stock,' Jesse Finch growled. 'We caught him dead to rights.'

'Then attacked his spread, shot one of his crew and strung up another. I heard about that. I also saw how his place was left.'

'That,' said Myrna McBride, 'was not our doing.'

'Then whose?'

Her frown was a mere twitching of arched eyebrows. 'A man like that is bound to have many enemies. Any one of them could be responsible.'

'Some of my boys hit Triangle,' Finch admitted. 'They tore up the place a bit, but they had no part in any lynching.'

He was lying, and having trouble with it. Trent turned back to Diamond M's owner, but her face told him nothing. 'The hell they didn't,' he muttered.

'They didn't.' Finch spoke as if he wanted no further argument.

Trent nodded slowly. 'And you think Baker was striking back? That's all you've got to convince you he killed your boss?'

'He was stealing from the Diamond.' Finch was trying hard to keep his anger in check. 'We proved that. Nobody else but him would have wanted to see McBride dead.'

'Will you tell me what you think you're hoping to achieve at Triangle?' Myrna McBride asked quietly.

Trent turned and started for the door.

'Where the hell do you think you're going?' Finch demanded, and when Trent stopped he was looking into the muzzle of a cocked .44.

Ignoring both the man and the gun, he asked, 'Changed your mind about me being a prisoner?'

Unaccustomed to having any man turn his back on her, Myrna McBride was on her feet, her face stiff with suppressed anger. 'No, you're free to go. But take this with you, Mr Trent: I'll not rest until Baker pays for what he did. I'll see him swing for his crime, and God help any man who tries to protect him. Do I make myself clear?'

'Very. But I think you're making a mistake about Jeff Baker.'

'No, no mistake has been made. Only

90

he had the motive.' So sharp was her response it could have sliced through rawhide.

Trent permitted a weary sigh. 'If anything happens to him — if your men try to carry out their own brand of justice, I'll come after every one of them. That's a promise. In the meantime, keep them far from Triangle.'

Carol McBride, that night wearing a white dress instead of the range attire she normally preferred, was walking back to the big house when the front door opened and a tall, wide-shouldered man came out and went up to the big red sorrel waiting at the rail.

As he swung the horse around, moonlight struck his face. Carol reached involuntarily for the arm of the man who walked beside her.

'What is it?' Hugh Beaudine asked.

'That man,' she said softly, feeling a strange disturbance as she watched him ride toward the wide gates, 'he was out at Jeff's — at Triangle.'

Beaudine frowned heavily down at

91

her. 'You were over there?'

She nodded, watching the departing rider, a dozen different thoughts tumbling through her mind. 'He said his name was Trent — a friend of Jeff's . . . '

'Carol,' Beaudine sighed. 'I thought you gave me your promise.'

She looked up at him, gently placing a hand against his chest. 'It's just that — the thought of him in hiding, not knowing what might — '

'Stop it,' Beaudine told her, somewhat harsher than intended. 'Baker's a killer; try to remember that. Whatever happens to him is what he's asked for.'

As he spoke the door to the house opened again, this time to release the stocky foreman.

Carol pulled away from Beaudine. 'Something's happened.' She took three steps, realized he wasn't following, and stopped. 'Are you coming?'

'You go ahead,' he said. 'I'd first like to have a smoke.'

She hurried to the house, passing Jesse Finch on the way. Beaudine took a cigar from his vest pocket and stepped over into the deeper shadows of the house.

'Well?' he asked when Finch reached him. 'What happened?'

'Not a damned thing.'

'What I thought.' Beaudine struck a match, touched the flame to the cigar and got it going. 'Mosley was hoping to square things, that's all — perhaps get his job back in the process.'

'The hell he is. Not while I'm ramrodding this oufit.' Finch paused, disliking having to look up at Beaudine. 'Lomax says this Trent's a bounty hunter.'

Beaudine blew smoke above the foreman's head. 'So that's it. I thought for a moment Myrna might have been hiring more guns.'

Finch didn't even try to keep the sneer from his face. 'What you mean is, hiring without your approval, don't you?'

93

'It was a thought,' Hugh Beaudine smiled.

'Dammit, Beaudine, all these guns — what for? We no longer need them. The Diamond's already bought up all the surrounding spreads.'

'Except one,' Beaudine corrected. 'The most important one.'

'So what? Unless Baker comes back the bank will foreclose. Miss Myrna can pick it up then.'

'True,' Beaudine conceded. '*If* he comes back. Then again, even if he does . . . Well, he won't live long enough to do very much, will he?'

Finch's booted feet moved uneasily. 'Things are moving too fast, Beaudine — going too far. When I threw in with you I never figured on getting involved in any killings.'

'That lynching still bother you?'

'Damned right it does. And I'll tell you something else that gives me trouble: Evan Lomax.'

'Oh?' Beaudine turned the cigar between his fingers, admiring the

94

glowing tip. 'I thought he was a good man.'

'He's a damned killer,' Finch retorted. 'It was him who led that raid, him who decided to use the rope.' He took a deep breath. 'Get rid of him, before he brings us real trouble!'

Beaudine laughed softly. 'Afraid he might usurp your position?'

Jesse Finch had no ready answer; he already knew that most of the present crew looked to Lomax for leadership. He looked away, over to the long bunkhouse at the far end of the yard.

'What you need to remember,' Beaudine said, this time his smile mocking, 'is that if not for your own enterprise, Jesse, we probably wouldn't even be having this conversation.'

He sauntered off, leaving Finch listening to the occasional raucous laughter that echoed from inside the bunkhouse, silently cursing Beaudine and everything that had happened since the lawyer's arrival in Twilight. All he'd needed was another year. After that

95

he'd have been his own man, the owner of his own well-stocked spread. Now, thanks to Hugh Beaudine, he'd be lucky if he was left with his skin intact. He swore again, and started off to the bunkhouse.

★   ★   ★

'Doesn't the fact that he murdered your father mean anything to you?' Myrna McBride, now experiencing some difficulty in maintaining control over her composure, stood once again at the head of the long table.

'I'll never believe that!' retorted her daughter. 'Not until I hear it from Jeff's own lips!'

'Perhaps you may still have the opportunity.'

Carol's green eyes flashed in anger. 'Not if those — men you've hired ever get to him! They'll hang him just as they — '

'I do not want to hear that from you again!' The ice was back in the older

96

woman's voice. 'There is nothing to prove the Diamond was responsible for that unfortunate incident.'

Carol shook her blonde head, her laugh soft but almost caustic. 'Oh, mother! We both know what happened! I heard Lomax joking about it. I heard — '

'Enough!' Myrna McBride snapped. 'This discussion is over!'

'It's what will happen to Jeff if ever he's found, isn't it?' Carol's voice was suddenly as cold as her mother's. 'They'll not even bother with a trial.'

The matriarch of Diamond M resumed her seat. 'One way or another he'll pay for what he did to your father.'

'And all because he refused to sell Triangle. Isn't that what started it all?'

'I said this discussion is over!'

'Why?' Carol wanted to know. 'What made father suddenly so land-greedy? We had everything, but suddenly it wasn't enough. Now most of our crew have left — replaced by men like Evan Lomax. Our resources are being

97

strained to the limit, but still you persist in — '

'Carol!'

The girl's shoulders sagged. 'I'm sorry.'

It was only a short moment in time that they stared at each other, but for both it felt like an eternity of silence. When Myrna McBride spoke it was with quiet concern. 'You're still in love with him, aren't you?'

Her daughter's head bowed a little, but she said nothing.

Myrna rose from the high-backed chair, went to her and placed an arm around her shoulder. 'He's no good, Carol. Forget him.' Her hand patted gently, consolingly. 'Try thinking of Hugh and how he feels about you. Hugh's a man of breeding; a gentleman — '

'Did I hear my name mentioned?' Hugh Beaudine asked from the open doorway.

Carol whirled around, a heavy blush flooding her face.

7

'What's wrong?' Evan Lomax grinned. "While back you were sounding off awful brave. Now I'm betting a hundred bucks and I don't hear a peep.'

Ike Mosley's face grew even redder.

Ben Keller scratched at the growth on his chin. 'This Trent . . . he fast?'

'Fast enough,' the skeletal-faced man answered.

'Faster'n you?'

Lomax broadened the grin. 'You hear me say that?'

'So why don't you take him on?' Mosley scraped back his chair, pushed up on to his feet.

'You making a bet, Ike?'

Mosley dropped the butt of his cigarette to the floor, stepped on it. 'You know damn well I haven't got that kinda money.'

A man almost as tall as Lomax, but a

99

lot heavier, with sandy-brown hair and sleepy eyes, got off the bunk on which he'd been sprawled. He opened his mouth to speak, but shut it again when the bunkhouse door was thrust open.

'Mosley,' Jesse Finch snapped from where he stood in the opening. 'Step outside.'

* * *

Trent took the horse into the barn, unsaddled and rubbed it down, feeding it oats after it was stalled for the night. His head still ached, and under the bandage on his arm the wound itched.

In the house he got a couple of lamps lit, a fire started in the kitchen stove, then sat back, waiting for the coffee pot to gurgle. He rubbed the back of his head, where the rifle butt had connected. Ike Mosley was still owed for what he'd done to the horse; now he owed him something more.

Rolling up his sleeve, Trent removed the bandage, found the wound had bled a little, but was drying fast. He balled up the soiled cloth and tossed it into the flames.

A cold wind touched the back of his neck. He stood up, suddenly uneasy in the quiet house, and moved quietly to the front room. Nothing stirred outside, but he waited at the patched window, eyes flitting from one point of the yard to another. From the kitchen came the sound of water boiling. A while more he waited, the feeling that he was no longer alone still with him.

A floorboard creaked.

Unsheathing his gun, he moved as silently as could be managed to the room at the back of the house. Almost at the door he was stopped by the sound of unconcealed movement.

'Come on in,' a voice called casually. 'Damn coffee's almost boiled away.'

Trent thumbed back the hammer of the .45 and stepped through the doorway.

'Hold it!' the man at the stove said. 'Put that thing away.'

A few years younger than Trent, he was well constructed, and without the dark growth that matted the lower half of his face would have been considered handsome.

'Surprised?'

Trent lowered the gun. 'A mite,' he smiled.

★ ★ ★

Ike Mosley was almost through saddling the steel-gray when the sandy-haired man came up behind him.

'What th' hell do you want, Alton?' he asked, making sure the cinch was tight enough.

Bob Alton shrugged casually. 'Tough, Jesse not taking you back, Ike.'

'The hell with him,' Mosley muttered. 'Who needs him? Who needs Diamond M?'

'Man carries a long grudge,' Alton conceded, remembering Mosley's drinking and the subsequent brawl that had got him kicked off the ranch. Damn, he'd just about stomped young Saunders' face in before Jesse stopped him. He had no liking for the man, but right then there was a way he could be used to profitable advantage. He said, 'You heard the bet Lomax made?'

Mosley snickered. 'Ask me, he's scared of that lousy bounty hunter. He knows he's trouble and wants someone else to snuff out his lights.'

Alton shrugged lazily. 'So let's do it.'

'You're crazy,' Mosley snorted.

'Not the way I got it figured, Ike. Besides, I pushed Lomax until he doubled the ante. That'd be a clear hundred apiece.' Alton's sleepy eyes drooped into slits. 'Care to listen?'

★ ★ ★

The moon was floating high when the riders pulled off the wagon road and moved into the cluster of pines. Ike Mosley remembered that this was from where that snooty McBride bitch had been watching when Trent had knocked

103

him on to his butt.

'We'll leave the horses here,' Alton said.

Still seething over the events at Diamond M, Mosley hauled his weight out of the saddle. Things hadn't turned out anything like he'd envisaged. At the very least he'd expected the boys to work Trent over until he told them what they wanted to know — giving him a chance to really bust a few ribs. But his chief hope had been for some resistance, that there'd be shooting and an opportunity to put a couple of slugs into Trent. Hell, he'd even imagined the boys getting mad enough to stretch his neck, to —

'Quiet,' Alton whispered as he tethered his mount. 'Quit the mumbling.'

Mosley tied the gray's reins to a low branch, turned and found Alton rubbing thoughtfully at his jaw, looking down on to the buildings below.

'There're still lights burning,' he said, telling Alton nothing he hadn't already seen.

'Up late,' Alton mused. Then his shoulders moved in a quick shrug. 'All right, so we'll have to change our plans a little.'

Still staring at the lamp-lit windows of the house, Mosley said, 'Maybe we oughta wait — do it like you said.'

'Yeah — maybe.' Alton got down on to his haunches. Lomax had been right about Mosley; the man was greedy for both money and a chance to even the score with Trent. And the plan he'd laid out was not only simple, but fairly safe. One of them would lure Trent to the front door while the other lay in hiding, ready to fire as soon as he showed himself. There was more, but that Ike Mosley would discover when the time came.

'Hey,' Mosley whispered urgently beside him. 'What if he's got company?'

Alton rose slowly upward. 'You think . . . ?'

In the pale light Mosley's teeth had a greenish sheen. 'If it is, we're gonna have a helluva lot more'n two hundred to split.'

* * *

Trent sat at the kitchen table, Jeff Baker across from him. 'You took a hell of a chance,' he said. 'They could have had the place staked out.'

Baker shook his head. 'They did, the first few days. Then I guess they figured I lit a shuck to a safer climate.'

Trent thought of the cigarette butts he'd uncovered, wondered if they'd been Baker's, if he'd established a stake-out of his own. But instead of asking, he said, 'They don't.' He gave a quick account of his visit to Diamond M. 'So why'd you come back?'

'Hell,' Baker smiled, 'after seeing you arrive and settling in, what'd you expect?'

Trent gave him a level look. 'Thought the girl might've had something to do with it.'

Baker toyed with the coffee mug, his

106

mouth tightening. 'For a time there I thought we really had a chance — in spite of her mother. Then every damned thing suddenly went to hell. Rory McBride got it in his head that the smaller ranches were becoming a threat to him. He started buying up properties. Those that turned him down he squeezed out; had their credit in town turned off, or gave them worse problems. Hired a bunch of gunslicks to back him. Wasn't hard, either. Drought we had here three years back crippled most of them. Time it was over they were just about broke. Me, I was lucky. I had water, not a lot, but enough to hold out and help where I could.' He pushed the mug aside. 'You still haven't said what brings you here, Will.'

'You really need to ask?' Before the question could be answered, he said, 'McBride also wanted your place?'

'After getting all those others he especially needed mine, and I'll show you why.' From a pocket of his coat he produced a thick wad of paper, unfolded it and spread it out upon the table, exposing it as a map on which certain areas had been heavily outlined in pencil.

A long wedge of land was identified as the Triangle. Abutting it, a portion many times bigger, marked Diamond M. Baker placed a finger on the map.

'All these now belong to the Diamond.' He indicated smaller sections that had been pencil-shaded. 'This here's mine. See how it stands between Diamond M and the others?'

Trent needed no further explanation. Without Triangle McBride's total holdings remained split. It was easy to see why he'd want to buy out Baker. He leaned back in the wooden chair.

'How about them claiming you've been doing a bit of night-riding?'

'Said the same thing of a couple of others.' Baker laughed harshly. 'Someone has, but it sure as hell wasn't me. Nor did I shoot McBride — in case that question crossed your mind.' He picked up his mug, took it to the stove. 'Hiding out's not the only thing I've been doing.' His voice became softer, more intense. 'I found out what's been happening; I know where their missing stock went . . . and now I got a few scores to settle . . . couple of debts to repay.'

Trent took it without comment.

Baker lifted the pot. 'More coffee?'

★ ★ ★

Alton had quickly become impatient to find out what was going on down below. Now, while Ike Mosley crouched in the shadows out front, he moved silently to the rear of the house, gun at the ready. Close to the lighted window he stopped, took a breath, then inched forward.

Two men, both holding mugs, stood talking, the tallest with his back angled to the window. Alton's mouth opened in surprise, closed quickly and twisted into a pleased smile as he brought up the gun, coming in still closer.

In the kitchen, Jeff Baker swallowed the last of his coffee, reached forward to dispose of the mug. Stretching past Trent, his gaze darted to the window. The coffee mug dropped from his hand, went skittering across the floor.

'Look out!' In a single movement he thrust Trent aside and grabbed at his holster.

Glass shattered, outside a gun thundered twice, sending Baker crashing back into the kitchen table. Trent spun, clearing leather as a third shot sent lead buzzing past his chest. He leapt to the left of the glass. His finger was again squeezing around the .45's trigger when he heard feet pounding in hasty retreat.

The first shot jolted Mosley where he was hunkered down safely behind a water trough. It wasn't how things had been set up; Alton wasn't supposed to — He shut off the angry thoughts as another crowded forward, and quite abruptly he knew with absolute certainty that his luck had changed.

Alton had seen an opportunity and grabbed it.

Mosley came out of concealment, a laugh rattling in his throat as more gunfire shattered the silence of the night. Already he could feel the money in his hand. He charged the house, going up the steps faster than he'd moved in years, hit the veranda, and went straight for the door.

It opened when he was still inches away, bringing him to a staggering halt. A strange sound croaked from his throat, his gun came up, and orange flame flashed from beyond the door. Hot lead bit into his side, driving him backward, firing as he went.

A figure, silhouetted by the light from inside the house, showed itself in the doorway. His hand frozen around the gun, Mosley tried to speak, but it was as if a rotting hide had been stuffed down his throat. He continued backward, head pivoting from side to side.

'No . . . '

Trent stepped on to the veranda.

'Drop it!'

Mosley's head continued to shake. 'No . . . For Gawd's sake . . . no . . . '

'Then use it.' The command was like the thrust of cold steel, churning up a sick sourness inside Mosley's stomach.

'Trent . . . no . . . ' Mosley's mouth worked furiously, but all he could muster was a thin, bleating cry. His right hand swung up, moving as if in a dream. Then with unexpected suddenness he lunged sideways.

He managed two wild shots before Trent, as cold as a well-chain, triggered the .45, slamming him hard against the railing. For a moment he clung there, slack-jawed, the gun growing heavy in his fat fist. Slowly his fingers uncurled, letting it fall. The hand moved up to his chest, came away wet, and Ike Mosley made one more tiny sound before his legs broke out from under him.

8

The town had been awake for less than an hour when Trent entered the wide main street, two riderless horses trailing behind the sorrel. In the darkness of early morning it had taken him a while to find the dun where Baker had said he'd hidden it; less time to locate Mosley's mount.

At a window in an office above Krieger's saddle shop, Hugh Beaudine, up earlier than was his wont, watched as the procession approached. He'd been thinking of the previous evening that hadn't gone at all well with Carol. The discussion between her and Myrna McBride had left the girl in a quiet, uncommunicative mood, completely unwanting of his attentions.

Then there'd been Lomax waiting for him in the shadows, eager to relate the plan he'd put in motion, of his

113

immediate anger upon hearing of it. The man's self-assured smile still lingered in his memory. 'Won't be no trouble,' he'd said. 'Once Trent is out of the way, Alton will take care of Mosley. It'll look like both came out on the short end of a shoot-up.'

He'd still been trying to fathom the man's motive, almost decided that behind it lay either a personal vendetta, most likely a fear, when Alton came tearing back to the Diamond with the news of Baker, of how he'd pumped two shots into him.

That had changed matters. Beaudine had almost congratulated the sleepy-eyed man, for now nothing stood in the way of Diamond M acquiring Baker's holdings. But until Trent appeared leading the horses, he'd still been host to secret doubts.

'He's here,' he said quietly, and Dix Miller rose from the deep leather chair in which he'd been lolling, and came over to join him.

Other early-risers had also observed

Trent's entrance. They stood on the edge of the boardwalk across the street, some displaying curious frowns, the rest, faces that were masks of clay.

Miller appeared slightly uncomfortable. 'Looks like Alton wasn't just whistling.'

'Better get down there,' Beaudine said.

By the time Trent dismounted, Dunn was already standing outside his office, waiting, eyes on both the slicker-wrapped burdens, and the group forming around the horses toting them.

'Want to hear it here, or do we go inside?'

Dunn jerked his head at the office.

Trent had about finished his report when the office door slammed open and the deputy sheriff stomped inside.

'What the hell's going on?' he demanded, round face tight, slightly flushed. 'Whose bodies are those?'

Bone-tired, his mouth tasting like the inside of an old grain sack,

115

and weary of talking, Trent slouched down in the hard chair, leaving the marshal to answer.

Miller pushed back his hat, rubbed at his chin. 'So Baker collected his dues, huh?' His hand dropped to his side. 'Him I don't care about. Ike Mosley, though, he's different kettle of fish.'

Trent looked up slowly. 'You trying to say something?'

Miller squinted down at him. 'Might be what I'm saying is, how are we supposed to know it happened like you claim?'

'Because I said so.'

'Yeah?' The sneer twisted the blond moustache into a crooked line. 'Now, I reckon, you're figuring on claiming the reward?'

Slowly, Trent unwound himself and pushed up on to his feet. 'Sonny, you want to forget you ever had such a thought.'

'Baker was his friend,' Virgil Dunn put in, trying to ease the tension starting to build in the room. 'You think it — '

The deputy swung on him. 'Keep out of this, Virg. This is business for the sheriff's office.'

'Then do something about getting those bodies off the street and moved to the ice house.'

Miller hesitated, his color rising. 'Watch him,' he snapped, and went outside where orders were yelled at someone in the small mob.

'Am I going to have trouble with him?' Trent asked.

'He's an ambitious kid,' Dunn answered. 'Uncle's the County Sheriff.'

The deputy came back in before any more could be said. Trent ignored him. Still looking at the marshal, he said, 'I want to make sure Jeff gets a decent burial. Who do I talk to?'

'Doc O'Conner. He'll take care of it for you.'

'Thanks.' He stepped past him to the open door. Miller reached out, grabbed at his arm. A pistol appeared in his right fist.

'Where the hell do you think you're headed?'

'To get a drink.' Trent looked down at the hand fastened to his arm, then slowly up into Miller's baby face. The hand fell away.

Again Dunn tried to relieve the strain. 'You said there was someone with Mosley . . .'

'Uh-huh. The one who bushwhacked Baker.'

'There's still only your word for that.' Though Miller's gun remained levelled, some of his cockiness had evaporated; he seemed unsure of what his next move should be.

'Tell you what,' Trent said, 'instead of overworking your gums, why not earn some of what the county's paying you. Take a ride up to Baker's place, see what it looks like.'

'Anyone can shoot up a place, make it look like — like what you said.'

'Yeah,' Trent nodded, 'they could do that. They could even leave boot prints under the kitchen window — and up where he and Mosley picketed their mounts.'

'How about it?' Dunn asked. 'If you want, I'll ride out there with you?'

'This don't concern you, Virg. Your job's here in town.'

The marshal shrugged. 'So I'll take the day off. What the hell, Dix — you'll need a witness . . . won't you?'

Trent smiled, said, 'Or are you going to let it slide, same as that lynching at Triangle?' and walked out of the office, without Miller making any attempt to stop him.

Someone had taken away the horses and the two bodies, but a small knot of the curious still remained. Trent had a boot in the stirrup when someone broke through the throng and again a hand took his arm, though this time very gently.

'Will . . . '

He freed his foot, released his hold on the saddle, and found Jean Arden peering up at him, blue eyes

119

wide and anxious.

'Are you all right?'

'Tired, is all.' He tried to smile, but it felt weak and forced.

'When I saw you ride in — those bodies — ' Her head shook as if trying to dislodge a grim thought. 'I — I didn't know what to think.'

'Jeff Baker's dead,' he said softly.

Jean Arden's lips parted soundlessly and in her eyes he saw something seen once before, a long time ago, and never forgotten.

'Someone else,' he said. 'Not me.'

It may have been there all the time, but only then did he see the tears streaking slowly down her cheeks. She reached for his right hand, took it in both of hers, wanting to say something, but not knowing what. The door to the marshal's office opened, slammed shut. Trent looked up to see Miller striding off, apparently in a hurry to get somewhere.

To Jean Arden he said, 'I need a drink, something to eat.'

'You need sleep.' She released his hand.

'That, too.' Uneasy under the stares of those watching, he forced another smile.

'Will . . . you said you'd be leaving soon.' She brushed at the moisture in her eyes. 'Now?'

Trent's face became grim. 'No, I'll still be around a while.'

'Don't go without seeing me. Promise?'

'I couldn't,' he said. 'Not now.'

As he spoke, at the far end of the street came the drumming of hoofs. In unison the small mob turned, hastily splitting apart as the calico came charging at them.

The rider pulled down hard on the reins, swinging out of the saddle before the pony stopped at the rail. Carol McBride, again in riding skirt and clutching a riding quirt, leapt up on to the boardwalk in front of the marshal's office, paused as she seized the door knob, flashing a harsh glare down at her audience.

Green eyes located Trent, fastened savagely on to him, and she let go of the door. With determined steps she came back down on to the dusty street. Jean Arden, realizing the girl was coming their way, moved aside.

Trent sought for words but was given no chance to speak them. The girl stopped in front of him, and he saw still another face stained with tears. A mixture of grief and untethered hate twisted her features, a strangled cry tore free from her throat — the quirt flew up, braked in mid-air, and come slashing down at him.

'You swine!' she cried. 'You *filthy, dirty swine!*'

9

Jean Arden let loose a tiny scream as Trent quickly shifted his head, grabbed Carol McBride's wrist, twisting it aside, pulling her still closer.

'Want to tell me what that was all about?' He plucked the quirt from her hand and let her go.

'You killed him!' The accusation was as cutting as a whiplash. '*You — killed him!*'

'No! Miss McBride — no!' Jean moved up to the girl but was angrily shoved away.

'If you're talking about Jeff,' Trent said, 'make sure you've got the right party next time you try using this.' He held the quirt out to her. When she ignored it he let it fall to the ground, nodded at Jean, and turned back to the waiting sorrel.

Carol McBride wiped the back of the

hand roughly across her eyes, watching blindly as Trent stepped into the saddle. She bent to retrieve the fallen quirt, straightening up to find herself confronting Jean Arden.

'I — I'm sorry,' she murmured.

Two men, standing at the back of the small crowd, waited until Trent turned the horse from the hitchrack, then broke away and started for the other side of the street.

'What you think?' asked the taller of the pair, a lanky individual with a dark drooping moustache and eyes older than the hills.

'Probably same as you.' His companion was stocky, broad-shouldered and slightly jowled. Both were dressed in worn range clothes; both walked as if all the time in the world was theirs.

★　★　★

Trent was on his second drink, his mind focused on the events of the previous night, and what Jeff Baker had

124

told him, when the batwings of The Avalon opened and a short number rigged out in a vest and a green eye-shade ambled in.

'Diamond M's just arrived,' he announced to anyone who might be interested, 'and Lady McBride's with 'em.' He strutted up to the bar, ordered a beer, gulped it down, and left.

Trent threw a casual glance over his shoulder. The saloon was just about empty, save for the old codgers playing a slow game of cards in the far corner, three men drinking in silence, and the two who'd come in shortly after him to take up positions at the far end of the long bar, They and a percentage girl who, attired in a gaudy kimono, sat alone at a nearby table, doing something to her nails, pausing every now and then to look his way.

Seemingly satisfied with her work, she gave her hands one final inspection before getting up and coming to Trent's side.

'Remember me?'

He looked down into a scrubbed, unpainted face which, in the morning light, looked hard and washed out. 'Am I supposed to?'

'Name's Rita.' She brushed at hair made frizzy and brittle by the heat of curling tongs.

He shook his head. 'Sorry.'

'Funny . . . you look real familiar.' The girl shrugged, showed a toothy smile. 'What the hell! I meet so many they all start looking alike.'

'Probably.'

'Want to buy me drink?'

Trent didn't want company, especially not now, not the kind she offered, but he called to the barkeep and put some money on the counter.

'New around here, huh?' She picked up her drink, another question already formed on her lips when the doors swung open to let in three more customers.

Evan Lomax was in the lead, followed by Bob Alton and Ben Keller. They took up places toward the end of

126

the bar, close to where the stubby man and his moustached partner leaned.

Trent swallowed what was left in his glass, made to leave, but Lomax's voice stopped him.

'Damn peculiar, that business at Triangle,' he said, presumably talking to the two flanking him, yet loud enough so all could hear. 'They're saying someone else was out there with Ike, but he's dead, right?'

Keller laughed quietly. 'Like you say, Evan; peculiar.'

'What I mean,' Lomax went on, 'with Mosley dozing in the ice house, now who's going to tell it different?'

Alton who thus far hadn't moved, turned to look down the length of the bar. 'Nobody, and that's the damn sorry part.'

In the corner, the old-timers put a hold on their game. The three standing between Trent and the Diamond M crew quietly picked up their drinks and found places to stand farther back in the room. The girl slithered away to a distant table, and a cloak of silence came down on the saloon.

Trent started for the door, but this time it was Alton's words which put a brake on his progress.

'Could be ol' Ike happened upon something at the wrong time.'

Trent detoured and walked slowly up to the trio. The sleepy-eyed Alton came erect; Keller and Lomax stepped clear of him. At their rear, two pairs of eyes watched with no apparent concern.

Trent was still yards distant when Keller yelled, 'He's going for his gun!'

Alton's right hand streaked to his thigh, snatched at the walnut butt poking above leather, got it halfway free and froze when realizing he wasn't going to have sufficient time, that a .45 was already levelling itself at him. To his right, Lomax, waiting for Keller's arranged call, had been faster. About to let the hammer fall, he felt something poke hard at his spine.

'Let's keep it fair, huh?' a quiet voice drawled, and Lomax, smothering a curse, lowered the gun.

Alton swallowed hard, uncurled his fingers to let the pistol fall back to rest. Both hands moved well clear of his sides.

Trent closed the distance between them. 'You were saying?'

Alton swallowed again, shook his head. 'Nothing.'

'Then let's keep it that way.' Gray eyes moved to fix upon Evan Lomax. 'How about you?'

Lomax holstered the gun, smiled thinly. 'Some other time.'

'Obliged,' Trent said, nodding at the lanky man standing behind Lomax.

He shrugged, put away his weapon, said, 'Time to be going, Shorty,' and came away from behind Lomax, making the batwings his destination.

Instead of following, Shorty took a path that brought him almost between Trent and Alton. He frowned up at the latter.

'Think I seen you before.'

'Go to hell,' Alton spat.

Shorty grinned good humoredly. 'Got a feelin' you'll be all settled in time I get there, mister.' Turning his broad back on Alton, he went to catch up with his partner.

Trent waited until they'd left before backing out of the saloon, the Peacemaker still trained on the three from Diamond M.

Once outside, he put away the gun, cast a wistful glance toward the hotel, and strode off in the direction of O'Conner's surgery.

The door to Hugh Beaudine's office closed and the lawyer stepped back to the window. Seconds later Dix Miller emerged from beneath the wooden overhang and crossed the street. Beaudine blew cigar smoke harshly at the dusty glass. *The young fool!* Instead of simply listening and leaving matters lie, he'd had to go and push his authority. No one would have given an iota about who had really shot Baker. If anything, they'd probably think his killer was deserving of the reward. Baker was, after all, supposed to be a wanted killer. But by shooting off his mouth, trying to implicate Trent, he'd perhaps given both the bounty hunter and the marshal something to think about.

He stayed at the window, remembering the day the sheriff's deputy had strolled into his office, grinning like an idiot. Still impressed with his appointment, Miller had spent three days trying to track down a cowhand who'd worked on one of the smaller spreads, who'd gotten himself tanked up and tried to rape the owner's daughter. By what could only have been a stroke of blind luck, on the third night of the wasted search, he'd spotted a rider he believed might be his quarry. It wasn't, but something about the man compelled Miller to follow. In doing so he discovered what lay on the other side of the Mule Heads, and beyond the barrens. Of even more importance, he was able to identify the rider.

What he'd not realized was that, by first coming to him, knowing of his association with Rory McBride, and no doubt seeking a good build-up from the lawyer, Miller had provided a means to hasten the process Beaudine had already started. When Miller left the office it was with more than some confusion; a man swayed by the lawyer's eloquence, clinging to the loyalty he owed the badge, comforted by the money nestling in his pocket, trying to see more clearly his position in the future Beaudine had painted.

Money and ambition had won over whatever loyalty Miller possessed, and he remained silent about his discovery. Only much later did he find out that old Rory McBride had not even been aware of the petty rustling. When, soon the raids on the Diamond's herds started becoming more regular, it was too late to backtrack. By then he was in the lawyer's silk-lined pocket.

The cigar had gone out. Beaudine found a match and relit it. Problem now, though, was that the kid had uncovered other things. Not only did he know far too much for his own good, but he'd begun to flex his muscles, believing himself to be a vital part in the scheme to take the Diamond.

The morning stage had arrived, and Beaudine realized he'd been watching the driver throw down luggage, the passengers alighting in front of the depot. He took a long draw on the cigar, was about to go back to his desk when he noticed one of the passengers come around the back of the stage, carrying a bag, walking in the direction of the Grand Hotel. A puzzled, slightly concerned frown rode up onto Beaudine's forehead.

Virgil Dunn, always around to see who got off the stage, had also observed the man in the dark suit, embroidered vest and narrow-brimmed hat. He'd seen him once before but still didn't know who he was or what business he might have in Twilight. He waited until he was a block off before pushing away from the wall against which he leaned.

Doc O'Conner had promised to take

care of Jeff Baker's body, to ensure it received a proper burial. He'd also insisted upon checking Trent's arm, and though satisfied it was healing rapidly, refused to let him leave without a fresh bandage. Something, Trent was sure, was on the little man's mind, but if he had questions he'd succeeded in keeping them securely under wraps.

Trent left, put the sorrel in the livery stable, and checked in at the hotel. He was almost asleep before he got his boots off.

How long he slept he didn't know, but when he opened his eyes the room was still filled with curtain-filtered sunlight, and someone was knocking hard at the door.

He swore softly, went to open it.

Standing on the other side, an overly fat man whose stiff collar was half hidden by a roll of fish-white flesh, said, 'Lady downstairs wants to see you.'

10

The hotel owner waited for Trent to get back into his boots, and together they tramped downstairs. Trent noticed Virgil Dunn relaxed in a chair close to the door, gave him a nod, and went over to where Myrna McBride and Charlie Thatcher sat in the farthest corner of the lobby.

Thatcher rose. 'You know Mrs McBride?'

'Please sit down, Mr Trent.' She waved a hand at the chair opposite her.

Thatcher smiled at the woman. 'Would you prefer to handle this in private?'

'No, Charles, stay.' Her eyes returned to Trent. 'I'd like to hear precisely what transpired last night — how Baker was killed?'

'Thought you'd have got that from the marshal.'

'I have, but I'd like to hear it from you.'

Trent shook his head. 'It won't be no different. Facts are still the same. Someone shot him through the kitchen window. Ike Mosley was hanging out front, to back the play.'

Myrna McBride's eyebrows arched. 'If it happened as you say, the reward I put up will go unclaimed. You're aware of that?'

Trent pressed back into the deep chair. 'That why you're here? To offer it to me?'

'If you've earned it — yes.'

They sat looking at each other; she waiting for his response, trying to read what lay behind the slitted gray eyes, he trying to figure what was going on in her head. 'You look like a well-bred lady,' he said slowly, 'so I'll make as if no insult was intended.'

'I'm sure Miss Myrna didn't — ' Thatcher broke off, nervously massaging his knee.

Taking his time to do so, Trent got

136

out of the chair. 'Little while ago your daughter appeared to be taking Jeff's death kind of badly.' He watched carefully rouged lips pull into a thin, slightly crooked line. 'Seemed also as if someone'd given her the same notion you have.'

'I'm not here to discuss my daughter,' she said tightly.

'Maybe not, but I think she's the real reason for this visit.'

Charlie Thatcher ran a fast glance from the woman to Trent. 'What's that supposed to mean?'

'Maybe she and Jeff once had plans.' A small shrug provided the rest of his answer. 'But this I know. Last night Mosley was out at Diamond M. Later, in less time than it'd have taken him to ride to town and back, he was at Baker's spread — with the one who killed Jeff.'

Myrna McBride's back stiffened.

'You want to give that reward to someone,' Trent continued, 'then check out your own crew.'

'Ridiculous!' The word was almost spat at him.

Trent's smile was bitter. 'It's going to set even harder with your daughter when she learns the truth . . . once she realizes you were the real cause of Baker's death. You and that reward. But if you can steer the blame on to somebody who's maybe hungry for easy money, that'd help a lot in making things right with her, wouldn't it?' He put on his hat. 'Just don't try using me, lady.'

'The man murdered her father!' What a moment before had been an uncommonly attractive face was now a thing drawn and ashen, suddenly aged beyond its years. 'He — he deserved to die. I — I did only what had to be done — to bring him to justice.'

His mien rattled, Thatcher got up. 'Trent — you've got it wrong. We honestly didn't — '

'Have I?' Trent turned his head to look back down at the woman having extreme difficulty in keeping her pale and slender hands still. 'Do like I told you, Mrs McBride, only do it fast. If I find him first he'll have no use for money.' He heeled around, walked away, glancing at the empty chair in which the marshal had been sitting.

Almost at the stairs, he stopped when Carol McBride came through the hotel door. She saw him, quickly averted her face, and went to where her mother and Thatcher still sat. Her eyes were red and swollen.

★ ★ ★

The man seated in Beaudine's office wore a dark suit, and an air of controlled anger. 'Damn it,' he said, 'we need Triangle. I promised our buyers a package, not split sections of land.'

'We'll get it,' Beaudine told him. 'It's just a matter of time now. Everything is —'

'*Time?* You've already had too much. You told us it wouldn't take long — no

139

more than a year. You gave us your word.'

'And I meant it.'

'Like you meant it when you promised 'till death do us part' to that lady now sitting alone in Boston?'

'Leave her out of it,' Beaudine scowled. 'She was one of my few mistakes.'

'Yeah? And this? It going to be another one?'

'No. You'll get what I promised. I've a stake in this too, remember? It's just taking a while longer than anticipated.' In an impatient sigh, Beaudine expelled his breath. 'If you think it was easy manipulating McBride, let me tell you it wasn't. That drought bit deeply into his capital. He got those other places dirt cheap, but he had to put up the Diamond as security when raising the loans to buy them.' He smiled. 'Everything is mortgaged to the hilt — his ranch, plus all the other holdings. And with only seven months left to meet those debts he was already falling behind with the payments. He meant to sell part of the herd to square things, but now that he's dead ... ' Still smiling, he laced his fingers together and slacked back in the swivel chair.

'After which,' his visitor said irritably, 'we'd buy up his notes and foreclose. I already know that.'

Beaudine lost the smile, freed his hands and leaned forward. 'And you also know that I've been taking care of the widow's affairs.' He paused, confused by the way the man before him lowered the lids of his eyes. 'Damn it, man, that foolish woman doesn't even fully realize the fix they're in — how much their stock has been depleted.'

'Doesn't she?'

Beaudine hesitated, frowned. 'Of course not!'

'Then tell me this.' Ice seemed to drip from his visitor's words. 'If she hasn't been buying back those mortgages, then who the hell has?'

It was a while before Beaudine could get his sagging jaw to work. 'What are you talking about?'

'You heard me.' The man in the dark suit rose to his feet. 'Why the hell do you think I made this trip?' Flattening his hands on the desk, he brought his face up close to the lawyer's. 'Been putting together some kind of double-cross, Beaudine?'

★ ★ ★

Though he tried, Trent was unable to get back to sleep. The anger he'd so far been able to keep under rein was rapidly bubbling to the surface, creating a restlessness, a need for answers to the mess Baker had found himself in . . . a need to do something physical. He lay on the bed, staring at the ceiling . . .

He recalled what Carol McBride had had to say about Jeff the day he'd met her at Triangle, and though he'd given no indication of having done so, he'd seen her on the arm of that eastern dandy the night he'd been forcibly taken to Diamond M. Yet Baker's death had obviously come as a hard blow to her. He thought of the way she'd struck out at him . . . then, without realizing it, he was thinking of Jean Arden.

He swung his legs off the bed, went to where his brush jacket was draped over a chair, searching the pockets for the map Baker had shown him. He studied it carefully, checking the reverse side in case notations had been made there. But all it contained were the pencilled outlines and names added to illustrate the extent and location of the Diamond and the surrounding spreads McBride had acquired. That and the tiny circle and arrow positioned at what appeared to be the foot of a hill or mountain.

A half-hour later, warbags slung over his shoulder, Winchester held loose in his left hand, he strode down the dusty street, heading for Engel's Livery Barn, hoping he wasn't about to waste time on a long useless ride, knowing only that it was something he must do.

In the shadow of The Avalon's

143

awning, Evan Lomax, Alton, and Ben Keller, waiting to escort Myrna McBride home, saw Trent step out of the hotel. Lomax dug an elbow into the sleepy-eyed man's ribs. 'Where you reckon he's aimed for?'

'How'd I know?' Alton replied, his tone surly.

Knowing that humiliation still seethed inside Alton, Lomax grinned. 'Still want to do it? Now's your chance.'

'You're crazy,' Alton muttered. 'In broad daylight?'

Lomax straightened up. 'Hell, you want, I'll even set it up — make it easy for you.'

Alton stayed silent.

'Or how about,' Lomax said quietly, 'I go over and tell him how Baker happened to pass away? Reckon that'd get you moving?'

Alton turned sharply on him. 'You're pretty damned anxious to have him dead, Evan. Why?'

'That's my business.'

'Then you do it.'

144

Keller chuckled. 'Whatsa matter, Bob? That jasper freeze your liver?'

Alton made a grab for the smaller man, but Lomax wedged in between them. Smiling at Keller, he asked, 'How's your liver, Ben?'

Yards from Engel's Trent heard his name called. Turning, he found Evan Lomax tramping quickly along the boardwalk. Caution set his hand to lingering at his holster as he waited for the skinny figure to step on to the street.

'Wanted to apologize,' Lomax said, coming up to him, smiling. 'Keller got spooked, thought you was going for your gun. Only reason I went for mine.'

'I believed that, I'd believe pigs had wings.' Trent swung around to continue on his way, hoping he was right in believing the skull-faced man wouldn't take advantage of his exposed back out where too many might see.

'Damnit,' Lomax called loudly, 'a man can make a mistake, can't he?'

Trent was in line with a narrow,

145

deeply shadowed alley when he stopped, started to come around, and changed his mind. Barely had he moved when a shot cracked the comparative silence of the town. Dropping the rifle, he went to the ground, pulling iron as he rolled.

Lomax's hands were wide from his sides when Trent came up on to his elbows, levelling the Colt.

'Hold it!' he yelled. 'Wasn't me!'

Another shot echoed from the alley, ploughing the earth inches from where Trent lay. Then came a scampering noise, the racket of crates overturning. Trent unwound up on to his feet, fired twice into the shadows, saw a dark shape appear briefly at the far end, and vanish. He lowered the gun, knowing there was no point in chasing, that whoever had been in there would be long gone the time he covered the alley's length. Holstering the gun, he walked slowly back to where Lomax stood, ignoring the people summoned out of the buildings by the noise of gunfire.

Lomax whistled softly. 'Must be born under a lucky star, feller. That was close.'

'And cute.' Trent's fist came up, found the point of Lomax's narrow jaw and sent him spinning. Spurs tangled, his body snapped back from the waist, twisted, and smashed into the dust of the street. Trent waited, anger riding his nerves hot and personal, almost hoping the man from Diamond M would go for his gun. But he lay there, unmoving.

11

That evening, Charlie Thatcher was the last to leave the hotel dining-room. He did so with reluctance, not wishing to return to a house containing all the comforts afforded by recent affluence, but which remained little more than a wooden shell, echoing loneliness from every corner.

A pity, he thought, that Myrna had gone back to the ranch instead of staying over in town, as had Carol. In spite of everything, they may still have been able to share a pleasant evening. There were so many things he needed to tell her, to explain . . .

He sighed heavily and started off along the boardwalk, remembering Myrna's arrival — the reception party a proud Rory McBride had thrown to introduce her to the citizens of Twilight. Charlie had been one of the guests, and afterwards he'd never been the same. A man who'd spent his life shying away from women, whom most thought of as a dyed-in-the-wool misogynist, Charlie Thatcher quite suddenly found himself completely smitten. Trouble was, two months earlier, during a trip east, Rory had already married her.

Charlie had been there when Carol was born; he'd seen her grow into a beautiful woman; he'd — He stopped at the door to his home. *Judas Priest!* Was that really *twenty-two years ago?*

In the living-room he poured a drink before flopping into a deep chair. Damn, but the leg hurt!

He swallowed the whiskey, cursed softly, bitterly, as still other memories came slowly drifting back.

Always, when visiting the Diamond, he'd cut a straight, short trail from his place. That day, six years ago, he'd done the same, unaware that Rory, in his haste to clear a small section of tree stumps, had elected to use dynamite.

The first blast went off as Charlie

was coming up the other side of a low rise. Stone, earth and timber fragments sailed through the air, raining down on him. Spooked, the horse lost its footing, slipped and went over . . . and Charlie was nowhere fast enough in trying to desert the saddle.

For two months he lay in bed waiting for the badly splintered leg to mend. For even longer he hobbled about, first on crutches, then a stick, gradually accepting the fact that he'd no longer be able to get around as before. Not long later he accepted Rory's offer and sold the Circle T.

He massaged the leg that still gave him much discomfort, the knee, which tonight ached with a vengeance, got up and refilled his glass.

Well, things hadn't worked out all bad, had they? He'd come into town, made a few investments, and before he knew it his capital had swelled by half. Then he'd bought a share in the bank, and though he didn't involve himself extensively in the day-to-day operations, it had proved to be an even more profitable venture.

He gazed about the room, at the luxurious furnishings, the costly drapes, the pictures which meant nothing at all to him, except that they looked impressive on the walls, and he wondered yet again if Myrna would want to live within these surroundings, or if she'd wish to stay on at Diamond M. He reduced the contents of the glass to half. Either way it made no difference, just so long as she accepted his offer. And Charlie Thatcher had every confidence that she would.

⋆ ⋆ ⋆

Late afternoon of the following day, like a giant barricade of sheer rock, the Mule Heads loomed up in front of Trent. Anything but a mountain, it was nevertheless too high, its sides too steep for a horse to scale. He sat slouched in the saddle, staring at it, well conscious that so far he'd been travelling mostly across Diamond M range, and was probably still on it, that if spotted by any of its punchers he'd have trouble on his hands. He nudged the sorrel onward.

A half-mile from the base of the ridge, he took the map from his pocket. The mark Baker had scratched upon it was obviously of significance. But what? He scanned the formidable rock face, stretching for miles in both directions, trying to locate the point the arrow indicated. A lonesome, dreary stretch of sand, scrubpine, outcroppings of boulders and scraggly brush, dotted with clumps of cactus and mesquite. After a while he headed the sorrel eastward.

Shadows were falling fast and it was starting to dawn on him that weeks could be spent here trying to find the meaning of Baker's mark. He paused to look back along the route he'd travelled, and that told him nothing, except that he'd probably gone too far. Bringing the horse around, he started back the way he'd come, weaving slowly through the tall brush and boulders. Against the graying sky a lone saguaro stood like a human deformity, its arms raised in supplication.

The sorrel lifted its head, nickered softly. Trent reined up, listening, hand resting on the butt of his Colt. Impatiently, the horse pawed the sun-baked earth. From some distance ahead came the faint, muffled clink of hoofs. Trent strained his ears, eyes shifting to every point of possible concealment, but it was as if he listened to the approach of phantoms. The hoof sounds grew louder, seemingly and impossibly coming from behind a dense cluster of cactus. He drew the Colt, moved the horse carefully forward.

Long moments later a rider came out from the other side of the cacti. Trent sat, unmoving as a second mounted man appeared, laughing at something his partner had said.

The lanky one was the first to realize they were not alone. 'Well now,' he said from behind the drooping moustache, 'looks like we got company.'

His partner turned faster than a man of his stocky build would have seemed capable of, grabbing for his gun as he moved.

'Hold it!' ordered the tall one. 'It's him.'

Trent moved up to them.

The stocky one relaxed and, grinning, let his hand drop from the gun butt. 'Howdy.'

Acknowledging the greeting with a curt nod, Trent allowed the barrel of the .45 to dip.

'Name's Mather. Called Shorty,' the lanky rider said, jabbing a thumb at his partner. 'Mine's Lafe Thompson.' His head tilted slightly forward. 'You're Trent, huh?'

Trent gave another nod. 'What's behind you?'

Lafe smiled. 'What you're looking for, I guess.' He moved his mount to one side, used his head to beckon Trent forward.

He went around the pair, stopping

154

when he was on the other side of the cactus that grew close to the base of the ridge. At first he could see nothing but rock face veiled in deep shadow. He went in still closer and one of the shadows appeared to grow even darker. From behind he heard either Thompson or Mather come up to join him, but he didn't look around.

'Goes right through to the other side,' Lafe announced when Trent stopped at the opening in the cliff face. It was dark and just wide enough for a single rider to pass through, an overlapping split in the rock which, just a few yards away would have gone undetected.

'And on the other side?'

'Place they call the barrens,' Lafe told him. 'Not fit to support a family of gophers. Stretches for nigh on four miles.'

Trent put away the gun, turned in the saddle. 'Going to tell me what you're doing here?'

Shorty who had moved up to join

them grinned. 'Trying to make up our minds, is what.'

Lafe said, 'We been ridin' with Baker these past weeks, ever since those Diamond bastards hit his place, planted that cow-stealin' on him.'

'Done us a favor once,' Shorty supplied. 'Figured we owed him a little in return.'

'How'd you know to come here?' Lafe asked.

Trent told about the map. 'This the route they've been taking the cattle?'

He nodded. 'Baker and us, we been keeping tracks of their movements, following their riders. Took a while, but eventually they led us right here.' Moving something to the side of his mouth, he sent a brown stream into the dust. 'How much'd he tell you?'

'Not nearly enough, but I'm starting to figure things.'

Lafe frowned. 'And what've you come up with?'

Trent took out the makings, shook tobacco into paper, tossed the sack to

Lafe Thompson, and told them. When he was through, Shorty was the first to speak.

'You figured right, mister. The Diamond crew's been stealin' their own stock. Matter of fact, some went through only this mornin'.'

Lafe blew smoke at the saddle horn. 'Few more weeks and they'll damn near have stripped the range.'

Trent took a last drag on the smoke, snuffed it out between his fingers and let it drop. 'You said there's nothing on the other side?'

Lafe nodded. 'Not for miles. But it's no big sweat getting cattle across. You do that you got no problem. And they had none. Got a bunch settled up in a basin half a day's ride from here. All the rest they moved to a spread in New Mexico.'

Shorty laughed softly. 'Nice, huh? This's the Diamond's north boundary, but seems even McBride hisself was ignorant of the way through to the other side.'

Lafe stiffened in his saddle, raised a hand for silence. Then they heard it too; the very faint, far distant echo of hoofs. 'Comin' back sooner'n I expected.' He turned a crooked, toothy smile on Trent. 'With a bit of luck you might just get to meet the jasper behind it all.'

★ ★ ★

Back in town, Hugh Beaudine sat with his feet up on the office desk, a drink in his hand, handsome face creased deeply in worried thought. It didn't make sense, none of what his visitor had told him. Worse, there was now some suspicion that he was pulling a double cross, and that they wouldn't tolerate. Before coming to Twilight he'd been paid a sizeable sum to do what he'd started, with a promise of a substantial share of profits once Diamond M and the surrounding ranches were sold in a package deal.

He emptied the glass, refilled it from the now half-empty bottle on the desk.

The only light in the office was that which came through the window, but the commencing darkness just then suited his mood. *Damn it, it had been his idea — he'd taken it to them.* He was the one who'd remembered their operation, who'd recognized the potential in what McBride owned — the weak positions of the smaller ranchers.

Beaudine swore loudly. It had taken time and patience, and a great deal of skilful persuasion to convince McBride that securing the surrounding ranches would not only establish him as a real kingpin in the state, but would also push up overall land values, making him an even richer man.

He'd gone so far as to arrange the mortgages through a Tucson bank, and only to appease McBride, to assure him of confidentiality, so that none in Twilight might know of his present financial status. But someone had, and that someone had acted before he and his New York colleagues could move.

He reached for the bottle.

159

Without those mortgages all his plans went up in smoke. If he failed to come across, his partners would not only want back their money, they'd probably also demand some form of retribution.

He swept his legs off the desk, stood up and carried his drink to the window. *There had to be a way out — to put everything back on track . . . There had to be . . .*

★ ★ ★

The light had all but vanished when the first rider came into the clearing, stepped his horse aside and waited. Presently two more appeared. From behind boulders, Trent and the men who had ridden with Baker watched. Some talk reached back to them, but it was of no importance.

One of the riders was turning his horse away from the others when Trent stepped out from cover.

'Lift them!'

The nearest of the three twisted

around, clawing at leather. His gun was well out when the Colt in Trent's hand bucked and knocked him out of the saddle. The one who had started to leave dug spurs, almost trampling Lafe as he leapt into the open. With only seconds to spare the lanky man threw himself to one side, skidding hard across the rough ground. Shorty let loose three quick shots. The first relieved the fleeing rider of his hat, but the others were wasted as he veered between brush and rock.

'Hold it!' a voice yelled. 'Don't shoot!'

Trent listened to the staccato beat of vanishing hoofs, closed in, Shorty following.

Lafe picked himself up from the ground, found his fallen gun, and approached from the other side.

It was too dark to see his face, but Trent had an idea he was smiling when he said, 'Step down, Finch. Got a gent here kinda anxious to make conversation.'

12

The beat of galloping hoofs reached Lomax while he was leaning up against a corral post, watching the light dimming fast across the rugged horizon. Grinding his cigarette under a boot heel, he started a slow walk to the gate.

Though still some distance away he recognized the horseman as Griff Santon, one of the pair who that morning had gone off with Finch.

'Where the hell are the others?' he demanded as soon as the horse was reined up.

Santon gulped air into his lungs. 'They got Brooker and Jesse!'

Lomax's insides went rigid. 'Who the hell're you talking about?'

'Trent an' two other waddies.'

'Get down,' Lomax snapped. 'Tell it slow.'

162

Santon slid out of the saddle, letting the reins fall. 'Damn, Evan, I could use a drink!'

Grabbing a handful of the man's shirt, Lomax jerked him up close. 'What the hell happened?'

'Told you, they was waitin' for us, this side of the Heads. Got Jesse and Brooker.'

'Dead?'

The man in his grip shook his head. 'No, but Brooker's been punctured. I hung back awhile, saw them movin' out.'

'And you? What'd you do? Light a shuck soon's the shooting started?'

'Dammit, Evan — I had to! They had us — '

But Lomax wasn't waiting for any more. Relaxing his hold, he shoved Santon away and stalked off to the bunkhouse, softly cursing the gutless wonders with whom he had to work.

★ ★ ★

163

Lafe Thompson and Shorty Mather rode on either side of Jesse Finch and the wounded Brooker, who sat bent in the saddle, his shoulder crudely bandaged. 'Awful quiet, ain't they?' Lafe remarked.

Shorty smiled across at the Diamond's ramrod. 'Reckon he's about all talked out.' He laughed, nudged his bay forward through the pale moonlight to join up with Trent, riding a little way ahead. 'Still figuring on taking them into town?'

Trent shrugged. 'Got no option.'

They rode on without speaking, the ground beneath them commencing a slow downward fall into a dry wash.

'Hope we're doin' the right thing,' Shorty muttered. 'I trust that squirt of a deputy 'bout as much as I trust grabbin' a cougar by his vitals.'

'Then you're not alone,' Trent smiled. 'We'll hand them over to the marshal. He can call in Miller after Finch repeats what he told us.'

'And he'll do what? Same's he did

after they hit Triangle?'

Trent said nothing until they were about to cross the wide stretch of sand and stone. Light reflecting off the opposite bank made everything seem brighter. Amid boulders and shale, stunted pines straggled up the slope, into a denser growth at the top. 'Back there you said you and Lafe were trying to decide something . . . '

Shorty tossed a quick glance back at his partner. 'They been to a lotta trouble tryin' to get Triangle, right?'

'So it would seem.'

'Well, now, could be they're figurin' with Jeff out of the pool there's easier ways of doin' it. Like when taxes roll around.'

Trent brought the sorrel to a halt. 'What are you telling me, Shorty?'

Mather shrugged. 'Hadn't got it all worked out yet . . . but maybe them cows they're holdin' in that basin oughta be worth a few dollars.'

Looking hard at the stocky man, Trent asked, 'Why'd you want to stick your necks out for something like that?'

Shorty stepped his horse around in a tight turn. 'Better have Lafe explain it.'

★　★　★

Nestled close to the earth behind a cleft in an outcrop of rock, Evan Lomax watched along the sights of the Winchester as the five riders began the descent into the wash. He wished Trent could know what was about to happen, and why it was happening. He wished there was time to remind him of Ezee Strachan, who'd refused to be taken alive and died under the bastard bounty man's gun. Ezee hadn't been much: a drunk, a man with few feelings, except where young Evan was concerned. A second cousin, that was all, but the only kin he'd known. He owed Trent for that.

Now he'd poked his nose where it didn't belong and he had Jesse Finch, who'd probably spill his guts under pressure. Topmost in his mind, though, was the burning memory of being knocked down and left cold in the dust of Twilight's main street.

The light was good and there wasn't much cover down there. He'd have no trouble picking them off. He shifted the rifle slightly, finger slowly squeezing . . .

One of the riders suddenly moved out from the rear, stepping his horse up beside's Trent's, shielding him from view. Lomax swore under his breath.

Again he shifted the carbine, this time lining it up on Jesse Finch. Maybe he'd already talked, but sure as hell he wouldn't be talking to anyone else! He squeezed off a shot and, without waiting to see the result, moved the gun again, and fired.

Shorty had only just pulled away from Trent's side when he heard the first crack from the concealed rifle, saw Finch thrust sideways from the saddle, Brooker following a moment later.

Lafe yelled a needless warning that was lost in the reverberating blast of

167

another shot, used his spurs, and headed for the left of the slope. Shorty pushed for the opposite direction.

Trent was spinning the sorrel around when two riderless horses came tearing at him, brushing by so close he had to pull hard to avoid colliding with them. A hot and furious breeze sailed past the back of his neck. Jerking the carbine from its scabbard he kicked the sorrel into motion, swung out of the saddle, hitting the ground at a run.

From behind a boulder barely big enough to conceal his body, Lafe was firing at a small ridge atop the opposite bank. He yelled at Shorty who'd found meager cover behind a cluster of backbrush, and then another rifle joined his.

The firing from above the other side of the wash came less rapidly now, each shot more carefully placed, each twanging off the rock behind which Trent was sprawled.

Three rifles sent lead tearing up at the crest of the opposite rise. 'Hold it!'

Trent shouted, and at once silence fell around them, leaving only the echo of gunfire still ringing in their ears. Trent waited, listening, thinking of the way Ike Mosley had laid for him, of the concentrated fire from the one now hidden up above them. No two ways about it, the gunman had selected his targets, almost ignoring Lafe and Shorty in his determination to first get him.

'Seems like he's quit,' Lafe called across the space separating him from Trent.

But still they waited, knowing that the lull could be nothing more than a trap, orchestrated to bring them into the open. Trent was the first to rise, moving cautiously into the shadows at his back, rifle tilted upward at the ridge.

'Gone,' Shorty grunted.

Lafe was beside Finch's body when they reached him. 'Clock's been stopped,' he muttered.

Trent took a look at Brooker.

'Wherever he's gone, he's taken along company.'

Rising to his feet, Lafe rubbed at his jaw. 'What now? We take in their carcasses, could be we'd have a rough time convincing anybody it wasn't us that killed them.'

Shorty swore, not bothering to keep his voice down. 'Dammit, just when things was startin' to break our way.'

★ ★ ★

Myrna McBride called to Lomax as he led the saddled horse from the barn. He stopped, letting her come to him. A handsome woman, looking even younger in the early morning light. Since signing on with Diamond M she'd barely ever spoken to him, except to give an occasional order, and since McBride's death almost all her communications had been directed through Jesse Finch. Lomax tried to keep the sneer from his pinched face. *Snooty bitch. Figures she's head and shoulders better than the rest of us.*

'Where is Jesse?' she asked.

'What I was about to go and find out,' he shrugged, and jerked his head back at the barn. 'Santon came in late last night — said Trent and two others got Jesse and Brooker. Few hours later, their horses rolled in. With empty saddles.'

With some satisfaction he saw her face go suddenly pale.

'I rode out to see if I could find them,' he went on, 'but it was too dark to do much. Now I sent a couple of the boys to check the east range. I'll backtrack north.'

'You — think something may have . . . ?'

He didn't let her finish. 'One thing's for sure. Those ponies didn't both lose their riders accidental-like.'

A hand flew to Myrna's mouth. 'Oh, my God. You don't think . . . ?'

Lomax nodded solemnly. 'Yeah. Maybe the same thing as happened to the boss.' He stepped into the saddle.

'I'd best be going.'

Myrna watched him ride away, realizing, not for the first time, how little she really knew of Diamond M's operations. Rory had taken care of that; he'd been content to have her as simply the mistress of his home, to look good for him when he returned at the end of a day's work, to share his evenings, to show her off in public . . . Now she had to rely upon people like Jesse Finch and Evan Lomax, and if something had happened to Jesse . . . There was the taste of fear as she recalled Trent's last words to her . . . She wished Carol hadn't stayed in town. She knew so much more about what was going on. Quickly she turned back to the big house, feeling as if she might be sick. As soon as he was out of sight of the ranch buildings, Lomax veered south, cutting a trail for town.

★　★　★

172

Hugh Beaudine's living-quarters consisted of two rooms in the rear of his office. That morning he awoke with a slight hangover, but also with a clear mind and an idea of what might lie behind his immediate problems. He walked to the hotel, sent a message up to Carol's room and invited her to join him for breakfast.

Most of the early morning crowd had already eaten, leaving them with the dining-room virtually to themselves. Waiting until they were served their second cups of coffee, he reached across the table and took her hand.

'Carol, there's something I must ask you . . . and I think you might know what it is.'

'Please, Hugh — not this morning.' Gently she extricated her hand from under his.

'I'm sorry,' he said softly. 'This isn't the right time, is it? It — it was quite insensitive of me.'

'It isn't just Jeff's death . . . ' She lowered her blonde head, a small shudder rippling through her body. 'Something's wrong . . . I can feel it . . .'

'Too much has happened, that's all.'

Her head shook. 'No, it's more than that . . .'

'Carol,' he said softly, 'I'm here whenever you need me. I want you to know that.'

'I — I do,' she murmured.

'It's the wrong time to discuss it, I know. It's just that I'd like to be sure you know how I feel about you.'

Carol pushed back her chair and Beaudine rose quickly.

'Have I said something wrong?'

Again her head moved in negation.

'No. I — I just have to see Dr. O'Conner, that's all . . . to make a few arrangements for — for — ' A tear spilled from her eye and she found herself unable to finish. 'Please excuse me, Hugh.' She turned, striding quickly to the door.

Beaudine picked up his hat from one of the chairs. Patience, he thought,

174

patience. But as he left the hotel he wondered why he was bothering. If the idea running around in his head proved correct, he wouldn't really need the girl; she wasn't essential. Still, it always helped to have a contingency plan . . .

In his office he was no sooner settled behind the desk when boots thumped hurriedly up the steps and the door flew open.

'Lomax . . . ?'

The skull-faced man shut the door and came to sink himself in the client's chair. 'We got problems, Beaudine.' He told the lawyer what had happened.

Beaudine leaned back, listening, his brow furrowed. 'All right, supposing Finch did talk. Supposing he told them everything. It would still be only their word. If he and Brooker are really dead — '

'They couldn't be any deader,' Lomax cut in.

'Then they have nothing to substantiate their claims.' Beaudine let out his breath. 'Somehow I don't think either

175

Trent or the other two you mentioned will come into town making any noises. If they did . . . there might well be some question as to who actually performed the killings.'

'Why do you think I sent men out searching?' Lomax grinned. 'They find those bodies, all hell's going to break loose.'

'Good,' Beaudine nodded, forehead creasing even deeper. 'Excellent. This puts Trent in a rather awkward position, wouldn't you say? In fact, I shouldn't be surprised if Diamond M felt justified in making another visit to Triangle.'

Lomax went on grinning. 'That what you want?'

'Yes . . . I think that's exactly what I want. Only this time make damned sure no one gets away. Wipe them out. Let's get rid of that little problem once and for all.'

13

The sun had marched high in the sky when Bob Alton came back alone to the ranch, leaving the two riders who had gone with him to continue the search. In the corral he found Lomax unsaddling his horse, apparently having himself just returned.

'Plenty of spent cartridges all over the place,' he reported, 'but not a damned sign of either Finch or Brooker.'

Lomax swore quietly. 'Should've figured he'd be too smart just to leave them there.' A moment longer he considered the situation. 'Get back into leather,' he told Alton. 'You're riding into town. Go to Beaudine. Tell him what you told me; find out if anything's happened since I left. Then get your tail back here on the double.'

The sleepy-eyed man sensed more

than simply concern for Finch and Brooker. 'Something going down?'

Lomax's thin mouth twisted tightly. 'Tonight we're riding on Triangle. And this time we don't leave a single thing standing — or breathing.'

If Alton had other questions he kept them to himself.

When he had gone, Lomax started for the house. Better let Lady McBride know, he thought, and now he was smiling. He had no idea what sort of game Trent was playing, but it didn't bother him overly much. So they didn't find the bodies. But that was all right. They didn't need them. Finch and Brooker were missing, and that was enough to justify the night's action he planned.

* * *

Beaudine wasn't pleased to have Alton calling on him. So far he'd been able to keep the Diamond's guns at a distance so that none might guess at any

178

connection. But too much else was on his mind right then to bother about such things.

'Tell Lomax nothing's changed,' he said. 'Just to make sure Santon's available when we need him.'

Alton came down onto the street, got mounted, and after only a moment's hesitation, turned in the direction of The Avalon. Wagons were docked at various points, horses stood at hitch-racks, but he paid them no mind. Not even the big red sorrel standing in front of the marshal's office.

Inside, Lafe and Shorty took their backs away from the wall as Trent levered himself out of the chair he'd been using. 'That's it, Marshal. Shorty and Lafe here can verify everything.'

That afternoon Dunn seemed to have added many years to his age. He rose slowly from behind the desk. 'Still wish you'd brought them in. Hiding their bodies in one of Diamond's line shacks . . . ' He didn't bother to finish.

'Place didn't look as if it'd been used

179

in the past year,' Lafe offered. 'Seemed a hell of a lot safer'n hauling them into town.'

'You're sure you never saw who did it?'

Lafe stroked his moustache. 'Like Trent told you, he was well hid.'

'One of those with Finch got away,' Trent supplied. 'Probably took word back to the ranch.'

'Right,' Shorty all but snarled. 'And they sent someone to set those two jaspers free.'

Trent had another idea about that, but he kept it to himself.

Dunn scratched his gray thatch thoughtfully. 'Pity Finch can't be here to tell his story. Might've been able to clean up the whole damned mess.' He brought his eyes to Trent. 'Let me get it straight now. It was him who started the rustling? He was setting himself up in business — had a small crew yonder the Mule Heads, to shift the beeves on to a spread he brought in New Mexico?'

'Been doing it for a long time, too,'

Lafe said. 'Shrewd cuss, that Jesse Finch. Made only small grabs so's not to raise any suspicion.'

'Until Beaudine stumbled over his scheme and turned it into something bigger . . . ' Dunn nodded, and kept on doing so as he turned a thought over in his mind. 'Starting to make some kind of sense now . . . McBride buying up all those other spreads . . . busting a gut to get Baker's . . . '

The others waited while he picked up a half-smoked cigar from the tin ashtray, struck a match and got it burning again.

'Fellow got off the stage yesterday, one I'd seen before. Checked in at the hotel, then went to see Beaudine. Name he registered under didn't mean anything, so I went up and took a look in his room.'

Trent remembered seeing Dunn in the hotel lobby when he'd come down to meet Myrna McBride and Thatcher. Now he knew why he'd been there.

'Not much in the room, but in his

181

spare suit I found some business cards tying him to a New York oufit called Colonial Land Investments. Imagine the name's not unknown to you. They buy up land and sell to foreign investors.' He blew smoke at the floor, gave Trent an up-from-under look. 'Now what business do you reckon he had with Beaudine?'

'I think,' said Trent, 'we're apt to find out pretty soon.'

'Which is what's been bothering me.' Dunn let loose a rasping sigh. 'Okay, until I hear it from another direction, I'll pretend to know nothing. Meanwhile, if I were you, I'd keep my back protected. Diamond ain't likely to take this sitting down.'

When they left the office, Trent paused on the boardwalk. 'You fellas get yourself a drink. I'll catch up with you later.'

Lafe raised an eyebrow. 'Yeah? And what're you fixing to do?'

'Pay a call on Beaudine. Put him in the picture — see if he reacts.'

Shorty, who'd been looking up the street in anticipation of resting an elbow in the saloon, said quietly, 'Remember, last night when we was talkin' and you said you wasn't leavin' till you had the one who bushwhacked Baker — either behind bars or inspectin' daisy roots?'

'I remember.'

'Told you while me and Lafe was cold-camped, waitin' for Baker to get back from Triangle, we seen this rider come hell for leather through the brush?'

'You saw him,' Lafe corrected. 'Time I got twisted he was long gone.'

'Yeah, well,' Shorty continued, 'seems like I'm seeing him once more.' He chuckled quietly. 'Thought I recognized that dozy puss.'

Trent and Lafe moved their heads to follow his gaze. Bob Alton had come out of the saloon and was standing on the edge of the walk, rolling a smoke.

'You're sure?' The question was Trent's.

'Sure's my socks got religion.'

Trent set off, angling across the street. Alton glanced up, saw him coming, dropped the half-built cigarette, and moved for his horse.

'Hold up,' Trent called. 'Some talking we've got to do.'

'To hell with you!' Alton spat back.

Those using the boardwalk swung about to look at where Trent had stopped in the middle of the street, then sensing trouble, quickly fanned out, well clear of Alton.

'To hell with one of us,' Trent said. 'Got someone here who says you were seen coming from Baker's place the night he was killed.'

'That's a goddamn lie!'

'Could be. So how about stepping over to the marshal's office and telling him so?'

From out on the street the raised voices carried back to Dunn. He went to the door, opened it, and heard boots clomping at a gallop. A third voice yelled, 'Trent! Freeze! You're covered!'

The shout surprised Trent enough to bring a sideways jerk to his head. Out of the corner of his eye he saw the deputy sheriff hit the street at a run, gun held tight against his waist. In front of him was more movement. He swung back to Alton, saw him suddenly leap away from his mount, a hand clawing at leather.

The gun came up fast, but he was rattled and fired too soon. The shot went past Trent's head, sparing him the split-second needed to whip out his own Colt. Alton's next shot struck the ground as lead punched a hole into his chest and sent him tottering. When he stopped his legs showed an unwillingness to go on supporting his body. He tried to bring up the gun . . .

'Son-of-a-bitch! Should've — killed — you — 'stead of . . . Baker. Should've — '

Then the hand that held the gun sank slowly to his side and he began going down to the dust.

Trent wheeled swiftly about, shifting

to the side as he went. But whatever danger had existed moments before appeared to have been defused by two men, a lanky one and a stocky one, standing some distance apart, blocking Miller's advance.

Trent holstered the Peacemaker.

Miller lowered his pistol and strode through the gap between Lafe and Shorty.

'You're in trouble, mister,' he said, smiling.

'Don't make a jackass out of yourself, Dix,' Dunn snapped, stretching up from his haunched position beside Alton. 'You heard him admit to killing Baker. So did at least a dozen others. You also saw who was the first to fire.'

Glaring at Trent, Miller put away his gun. 'All right; I heard.'

'Then,' said Trent, 'we have no further business, do we?' He turned to his partners. 'Get your drinks. What I've got to do won't take long.'

★　★　★

186

Since arriving in Twilight, Hugh Beaudine had never before spent so many straight hours at his desk. Only when he'd heard the commotion on the street had he moved, and then but to the window where he was unable to see what was happening. Now, hearing the footsteps ascending the wooden steps, he fully expected to find Dix Miller come bearing news. But it was Trent who came into the office.

'Something I can do for you?' He frowned, unable to think of any reason for such a visit.

'Other way around. It's what I can do for you.'

Beaudine sat up straight. 'Then — take a seat.'

'Prefer to say this standing.' From his shirt pocket Trent took the makings, dawdling over the shaping of a cigarette. 'I know how Diamond M's beef went, and where they went. Believe I might also know what's behind it all. In other words, I've got your number.' He put away the Durham sack, licked the

187

paper. 'Colonial Land Investments, huh?'

'Am I supposed to know what you're talking about?' The quaver in the lawyer's voice betrayed the question.

'Uh-huh.' Trent fished out a match. 'What I'm here for is to tell you to keep your dogs hell and gone away from Triangle.'

'Have you gone crazy? My — *what?*'

'You heard me.' Trent scratched the match against the surface of the polished desk, touched the flame to the cigarette. 'Lomax, Alton — now deceased — and the rest of that bunch at the Diamond, they're all in your pocket.' He let the match fall to the floor. 'Now listen carefully, Mr Beaudine, because I'd hate you to make any mistake about what I'm saying. Jeff Baker took care of a couple of things before he cashed in. Like drawing up an agreement which says that should anything happen to him, a man named Lafe Thompson, and another called

188

Mather, inherit Triangle, lock stock and barrel.'

'Rubbish!' Beaudine flared. 'Such a document would never be considered legal.'

'Don't put money on it. It's hand writ and independently witnessed. Any court will honor it.'

Beaudine sucked in his breath. 'Very well. If that's all you've come to say, allow me to appraise you of a couple of things.'

Trent waited while Beaudine picked up a silver sword-shaped letter-opener and began cleaning his spotless nails. 'I'm told that two men are missing from the McBride ranch, Jesse Finch being one of them. More importantly, there is a witness — fellow called Santon — who is ready to testify that when last seen they were being held captive by you.' He tossed the letter-opener on to the desk. 'So here's some free advice. By tonight, either release both, alive and well . . . or I'll request the sheriff's office to take action.' His smile became

189

that of someone holding all the aces. 'Do we understand each other?'

'No question of it.' Gray eyes narrowed. 'Keep your dogs away, Beaudine. I won't be telling you again.' He went to the door, opened and held it. 'That why McBride had to die? Because he also tumbled to your game?'

'If you're leaving,' said Beaudine, the smile despatched to oblivion, 'don't let me detain you.'

With Trent gone, he sat for a long time in stony silence. Then he pushed up and away from the desk, plucking a .38 calibre revolver from its armpit holster, checking the cylinder to make sure it was fully packed. The fury raging within him brought a trembling to his hands. Pointing the gun at the closed door, he let his curses ring loud in the small office.

After a while he holstered the pistol and brought out the bottle. Very well! Too much was breaking into the open. Very possibly Trent had taken his information to the marshal — but so what? They still lacked proof, and by the time they got it — *if they got it* — it would be too late. He gulped down the drink, refilled the glass. All it meant was that he'd have to move a little faster. Nothing was yet lost. But, by damn, the man would pay! He'd rue the day he rode into Twilight!

* * *

On his way to meet Lafe and Shorty, Trent slowed up in front of Jean Arden's Fashion Shop, checking through the window, to make sure there were no customers present before going in.

Jean looked up from the catalog she was reading. 'Will — ' She came out from behind the counter, conjuring up a small nervous smile.

Suddenly he regretted his decision to stop, not sure now why he had. She didn't have to say anything to let him know she'd either witnessed or been told of the incident with Alton. He'd

191

seen that look before.

'Oh, Will . . . ' She moved quickly, and his arms were waiting willingly to enfold her. Cheek pressed tight against his chest, she clung almost desperately to him. 'Will — what's happening . . . ?'

'Nothing that won't be cleared up pretty soon.'

Her head moved away so that she might look up into his face. 'Is that why you really came here?'

'Told you the reason,' he said. 'Before that I had no idea of Baker's troubles.'

'And now . . . that he's dead?' Her arms fell away from him and he let her go. 'The man you shot, was he the one who . . . ?'

'A hired gun, that's all.' He looked away, through the window, and saw the light fading, wishing again that he were somewhere else. This was too much like a repeat performance of another time that had taken too long to forget. He sighed softly. 'I'll be going.'

The blue in Jean's eyes began to

cloud. 'No, Will — don't.'

'Seems like we've had this discussion before,' he murmured.

She nodded. 'And I was wrong.'

'Were you, Jean?'

Another nod, and now her lower lip trembled. 'I was afraid . . . too stupid to realize you were only doing a job few others would take.'

'Nobody's paying me now,' he said. 'What sort of difference does that make?'

She tried to speak, but the quiver in her lip only got worse. Tears began to tumble, and in a moment she was again clinging to him, sobbing, holding so tight he could almost feel the beat of her heart.

* * *

When he arrived at The Avalon, Lafe and Shorty were on their fourth drink. He moved in silently beside them, signalling to the bartender.

'What's gnawing at you?' Lafe

193

frowned. 'Looks like you just lost your reason for living.'

Trent put money on the counter and picked up his drink. 'Or found it,' he said. 'I'm not sure.'

14

Ben Keller was waiting for Lomax when he came out of the house. 'What she say?'

'Says to leave it to the law.'

'You tell her about them finding Finch and Brooker in that line shack?'

'Also told her the crew's pretty riled,' Lomax smiled. 'Lady's taking it bad. Wants someone to go and fetch the daughter home.'

Keller appeared disappointed. 'That mean you're calling it off?'

'Hell, Ben, you seen how worked up them boys are. Don't reckon anything'll stop them now, do you?'

'Not after that little speech you gave them.' Keller grinned. 'Okay, so what're we waiting for?'

'Take it easy.' Lomax started walking away. 'It'll be dark soon.'

'How about the girl? You sending for her?'

Lomax stopped. 'Well, sure. Orders is orders. When we're through you can have the honor.'

'And her?' Keller nodded toward the house. 'What'll she do after she finds out?'

'Like I said, Ben, orders is orders. Why, man, you were right there with me, weren't you? You heard her order us to hit Triangle, to get the ones that killed Jesse and Brooker.' Laughing softly, Lomax continued on his way.

* * *

Pacing the floor of his office, his mind working overtime, Hugh Beaudine also waited for darkness. All day he'd been trying to reason out recent events, and now he was positive that he had the answers. Not only did he know how he'd secure Diamond M and its other holdings, but also how to get Trent out of the way . . . to smash Triangle in the process. After that he'd have only to pick up the pieces, tie everything into a neat package, take his pay-off, and head for more lucrative territory.

* * *

In The Avalon Saloon, Lafe said, 'Something sure as hell's troubling you.'

Trent shrugged. 'Maybe a couple of things.'

Shorty laughed softly. 'Woman problems!'

'Yeah ... ' A small twinkle popped into Lafe's eyes. 'We seen that little lady — the way she was bawling all over you, after you brought Baker and Mosley in.'

'Pretty, too,' Shorty put in.

The smile Trent tried didn't come off. Anxious to change the subject, he said, 'Listen, I need to see the marshal. How's about I meet you later and we'll put on the feedbag?'

'Well, now,' Lafe answered, 'me and Shorty been talking. Figured on one more drink then going out to Baker's spread.'

Trent frowned. 'Moving in?'

'Assuming that paper's legit.' Lafe hesitated. 'Yeah . . . before someone else gets the same idea.'

'May need to be Okayed by a court, and registered,' Trent told him, 'but I don't think you'll have any problem.'

'Other thing,' Shorty said, studying the contents of his glass, 'is you. Way we see it, you and Baker were long-time pals. So you want to come in with us, you're welcome.'

'Equal shares,' Lafe added.

Trent looked from one to the other, not sure what to say. 'That's mighty generous, boys. But I've a place waiting. Soon's all this is over I'll be heading home.'

Lafe shrugged, knocked off the rest of his drink. 'Offer stands.'

'And it's appreciated.' Trent emptied his glass, deposited it on the bar. 'Don't know about you, but I'm starving.'

★ ★ ★

It was dark when, an hour later, Trent went over to the marshal's office.

'Might be a good idea having them there,' Dunn said after being told that Shorty and Lafe were riding to Triangle, intending to move in. 'Only hope they know what they're taking on. It's going to need work gathering what stock's left, fixing up the place, and' — he picked up his cigar, took a few puffs giving Trent a somewhat curious stare — 'taxes'll be coming around soon.'

'I've a feeling they'll manage. They're no fools.'

'But,' said Dunn, 'that's not why you're here, is it?'

Trent started building a smoke. 'Hoped you could tell me something more about the way McBride got it.'

Dunn blew smoke at the desk, shrugged. 'Not a lot to tell. His mount came in late that afternoon, without him. They sent out searchers, but it

199

wasn't till the next day he was found.'

Trent lit the cigarette. 'Where was that?'

'Along the pass, bottom of Eagle Claw. Body was tucked in between rocks and a tangle of brush. Might've stayed there a lot longer weren't for a couple of buzzards thinking on filling their bellies.'

'Shot in the back, right?'

Sucking on the cigar, Dunn nodded. 'Why the questions?'

'Don't know,' Trent replied honestly. 'Maybe I'm just trying to get the full picture. Maybe trying to ease an itch . . . remember something.' He looked at the glowing tip of the cigarette as if hoping to find another answer there. 'Everybody who's told me about it said Baker was the one who shot him. Jeff denied it — and I believe him.'

'Wish I could help, but it wasn't me who handled it. Miller took care of that. Way he puts it together, Rory was dismounted when he met up with someone. Something went wrong and he tried to find cover behind those rocks. Only he was too slow.'

* * *

Charlie Thatcher, his coat discarded, vest unbuttoned, and whiskey riding heavy on his breath, closed the door and, in a manner which made no effort to conceal his displeasure, scowled up at his visitor. Never before had Beaudine called upon him and he didn't particularly welcome him doing so this night.

'Nice,' said Beaudine, glancing around the wide entrance hall, strolling casually through to the lavishly furnished living-room. 'You've been doing all right, Charlie.'

'What the hell are you here for?'

Beaudine came slowly around. 'Heard a little story, yesterday, Charlie. Fellow told me McBride put up Diamond M for security on loans.'

Thatcher snorted irritably. 'If he did, it's news to me. Anyway, he sure as hell

201

didn't do it through our bank.'

'No,' Beaudine agreed, 'he didn't. He went to Tucson for that.'

'So he went to a Tucson bank. How does that concern me?' Thatcher's irritation was rising fast.

'Charlie, Charlie . . . let's not waste precious time.' Beaudine smiled patronizingly. 'Someone got wind of McBride's transaction and started buying up his paper . . . and we both know who that was, don't we?'

'Get your butt the hell out of here!' Thatcher said tightly. 'And take your stinking accusations with you!'

Beaudine didn't move. 'Come now, Charlie. You're the only one I can think of who might have a contact in Tucson — someone who'd tip you off on what was happening. Moreover, you're the only person I can think of with any motive.' He widened the smile. 'You see, Charlie, I've seen you with Myrna McBride — seen that puppy dog expression you wear whenever she's around.'

Thatcher's anger suddenly exploded. 'Why, you filthy — ' His fist came up, but Beaudine simply stepped back and the momentum of the intended blow almost sent him sprawling. Regaining his balance he whirled again upon the lawyer, stopping abruptly upon finding himself staring into the muzzle of a nickel-plated gun.

'What's more,' Beaudine went on as if nothing had happened, 'I'm aware of your accident — and how it was caused. You never let on, but you hated McBride for that, didn't you?'

'Get out of my home!' Thatcher said through teeth clenched so tight his jaw hurt. 'Get out!'

'No, Charlie. Not until I get what I came for.'

Thatcher looked at him stupidly.

'The papers, Charlie. The mortgages. What you're going to do is sit down and sign them over to me.'

'You're crazy! Who says I've got — '

'Don't waste my time,' Beaudine's voice cracked harshly, cutting off the protest. 'Either do as you're told or I call in our young deputy sheriff and tell him everything. Who knows that quite possibly he'll put two and two together — and arrive at the same answers I have.' The smile was slowly resurrected. 'Exactly why did you kill McBride, Charlie?'

★ ★ ★

From the window of her hotel room, Carol McBride stared vacantly down on the street below. Most of the afternoon she'd sat there trying to make sense of all that had happened. Until the news had come of Jeff's death she'd continued, in spite of every opposing opinion, to believe in his innocence, that he'd be able to vindicate himself and all would again be as it once was. But that dream was ended now, and tomorrow she'd be placing flowers on his casket.

She thought she'd emptied herself of tears, but they came again, blurring her

204

vision, trailing warmly down her cheeks. Why hadn't she turned her back on the advice and persuasion of her mother? What if she could have found someone more polished, of better standing than Jeff? It wasn't what she wanted. Already she'd found the man with whom she was prepared to share her life. Then why hadn't she simply married Jeff when he'd asked her? Perhaps if she'd done so none of this would have happened. Perhaps. She got up, found a fresh handkerchief and dabbed at her eyes.

The walls of the room seemed to tilt at her, the air began to taste thick and stale. She moved to the door. She had to get out . . . talk to someone . . .

★   ★   ★

Charlie Thatcher felt cheated, humiliated, and more than a little afraid. Beaudine had guessed right. Everything he'd done had been for Myrna. If he owned the Diamond he'd win her over,

205

of that he'd been positive. And then Charlie remembered something which had become swamped under the recent barrage of dreams he'd been harboring. It hadn't really started out that way, had it?

When his contact at Tucson wrote him about McBride's dealings he'd immediately seen an opportunity to hit back at Rory — not merely for the accident which had crippled him, but also to render him useless in the eyes of Myrna. Vengeance had been at the core of everything. He remembered how he'd laughed when finding out about Diamond M being mortgaged. Ironic, wasn't it, that Rory, by using that damned dynamite, had placed him in a position to get rich . . . rich enough to buy up his notes.

Seated at a small writing desk, he signed his name for the last time, and put down the pen. But then Rory, too, had contacts. Damn fool! He'd picked up his mail that day and, after reading the letter containing the tip-off, had gone straight to his old friend Thatcher. Charlie, he'd figured, could find out who was behind it. Trouble was, he'd hoped to keep it all under wraps until the time suited him for a final showdown, and now, one way or another, Rory was going to eventually learn the truth. When he did, Charlie Thatcher's life wouldn't be worth spit.

But he'd never been accused of being slow of mind. He knew of the trouble that had flared up between Diamond M and Triangle, that they were still hunting Baker, going to do God knew what when they caught him. All of it suited him more than nicely. In fact, it made everything so much better. This way there'd be no more waiting. He saddled up, left Rory in town to attend to whatever other business he'd had, and rode off to wait at that little park near Eagle Claw.

'Finished?'

Instead of answering, Thatcher gathered up the papers he'd endorsed and, twisting around on the hard-backed

207

chair, held them out to the lawyer.

Beaudine flipped through the documents, while Charlie watched, seeing all his plans, all the money he'd invested, being snatched from him by this grinning dandy. He saw too that the gun had shifted, was no longer pointed at his head . . . and Beaudine was not even watching him.

Charlie's hand moved stealthily to the upper left drawer in the desk, began sliding it open. Under his fingers he felt the cold metal of the old Navy Colt.

'We'll keep this between ourselves, won't we, Charlie? Anyone needs to know, you were acting as my agent.' He was folding the papers when two things happened simultaneously. He heard the rattle of the door knocker, saw Thatcher swivel sharply around, the thing in his hand coming up fast.

He dropped the papers, shoved his own right hand forward, triggering the gun when it was scant inches from Thatcher's head.

Shaking, he stared down at the old

man thrown from the chair, crumpled on the floor, the hideous thing that had once been a face.

'Uncle Charlie . . . ?'

Beaudine's feet refused to function; it was as if paralysis had taken possession of his body.

'Uncle Charlie . . . ?' Nearer now . . . nervous and worried.

He remembered the sound at the door, realized she'd heard the shot and was coming in . . .

Somehow he found the will to move, and when Carol stepped into the room he was concealed at one side of the door.

She saw the body on the floor, took a forward step, hand flying to her mouth. Before she could scream Beaudine's gun was smashing down at the back of her head.

★   ★   ★

As he walked the sorrel along the street of houses placed in no particular order,

209

Trent was thinking of the day Charlie Thatcher had picked him up and brought him to town. Along the way they'd talked of Jeff Baker's problem . . . McBride's death. *Met up with him at a little park near Eagle Claw.* Thatcher had told him. *Pumped two bullets in his back then tried to hide the body.* It probably meant nothing, but it seemed to be more than anyone else knew. And Thatcher was connected with the local bank. He'd be ideally situated to find out about McBride's dealings, and according to Dunn, not without substantial funds. Enough to buy up McBride's mortgages?

Ahead he saw the house Dunn had described. It stood distant from the others, tall, proud and impressive. Trent nudged the horse to a quicker pace, dismounted at the white fence and tossed the reins around a picket.

Light glowed brightly in the downstairs windows, so Thatcher was obviously home. Trent was reaching for the knocker when he got the first whiff of smoke. At the nearest window, he saw the light bright and flickering. Seizing the door handle, he pushed inward.

'Thatcher?' he shouted.

As if in answer to his call, from an open door at the end of the hall, a thin odorous cloud rushed out to greet him. Beyond, a tall, hazy figure appeared. Trent made to call again when there was a sharp, cracking report followed by a lance of flame hurtling through the rapidly thickening gray veil of smoke. Something struck his head, and then it felt as if the roof of the house had come crashing down upon him, obliterating everything.

★ ★ ★

At the Diamond M, Evan Lomax, Ben Keller and a crew of six were getting saddled up. Myrna McBride watched through a slit in the curtain, and for the first time in years sought help in prayer.

15

They hit the ranch in a straight frontal attack, disregarding stealth in the belief that Triangle would either be deserted, or, as Lomax hoped, they'd have only Trent and that mis-matched pair to contend with.

Crossing the yard from the barn, Shorty was the first to hear them. 'Trouble coming!' he yelled, sprinting for the bunkhouse.

Lafe already had his carbine ready and was dousing the lamp when Shorty entered. 'Sounds like they brought every damned hand along.'

Shorty grabbed up his rifle and went to a window. 'Let the bastards come. Maybe we can give 'em somethin' they ain't bargained for.'

'What I always liked about you,' Lafe said, taking a position at another window. 'Forever the optimist.'

At the crest of the wagon road, Lomax pulled rein, raising a hand for the others to stop.

Ben Keller came in at his side. 'Don't seem like anybody's home.'

'Either that or they're already turned in.' Lomax twisted in the saddle to face those behind. 'All right. We go in fast. Give them everything we've got.' He turned back, smiling down at the darkened buildings. 'If they're there, that'll stir them.'

'Here they come,' Shorty said, as the first riders came charging down the road, firing as soon as they reached the yard.

'Hold it,' Lafe murmured, watching them mill around the house, dispatching lead at the windows and door. 'Let them enjoy themselves a while.'

'There's that Lomax, right smack in the middle of the pack,' Shorty observed, the muscles around his mouth tightening hard.

Lafe smiled to himself. It was only natural that Lomax would believe they'd make use of the main house. Probably never gave a thought to the fact that men such as he and Shorty might feel a bit uncomfortable moving in where everything had been personal to Baker, that they were more at home where they'd hung their warbags. 'Okay. Now!' His trigger finger started to tighten.

A rider, positioned close to Lomax, quite unexpectedly lifted out of the saddle. Above the racket of blazing guns he heard someone swear loudly. 'The bunkhouse,' yelled another. 'They're in — ' and a shot, its sound lost in the noise of too many others, never permitted him to finish.

'Scatter!' Lomax shouted, sending his mount charging for whatever protective cover might be found around the side of the house.

'Lookit 'em skeedaddle!' Shorty laughed, firing at a Diamond M hand who moved just in time to save himself from a fast trip to hell.

'Yeah,' Lafe muttered. 'And now our

214

troubles only start. Be a lot tougher picking them off now they know where we are.'

'There's two that won't be doin' a damn thing, that's for sure.' Shorty peered across the yard, trying to locate a target. But the moon had slipped behind a cloud, making it difficult to see much.

Lafe was silent for a while. Then he asked, 'How many shells you got?'

Shorty's sigh hissed through the dark. ''Fraid you was gonna ask that.'

'Yeah,' Lafe grunted, 'and a bit late to go shopping now.'

★ ★ ★

The bottle was again on Beaudine's desk, close by a thin leather case in which he'd placed the papers taken from Thatcher. Sickness still welled about in the lawyer's stomach, sapping his handsome face of color. He'd killed men before — two of them — and it had never caused him any loss of sleep.

215

Nor did it bother him having to kill Thatcher and Trent. But Carol . . . that was different. Leaving her to die in those flames . . . He was pouring another drink, when the door opened to let in Dix Miller.

Beaudine cursed under his breath. He hadn't even heard Miller coming up the steps, and right now he had no need of the idiot's company.

Miller looked at the bottle. 'Private party?'

There was in the deputy's attitude something that caused Beaudine a certain uneasiness. 'Want something, Dix?'

'Charlie Thatcher's house is burning,' Miller told him, and now he was frowning.

Beaudine shrugged. 'Such things happen.' From a desk drawer he produced another glass. 'Sit down. Might as well have a drink seeing as you're here.'

Miller remained standing, brow deeply ridged. 'There's the stink of smoke . . . coming right from where you're sitting.'

Beaudine tilted the bottle. 'You're imagining things.'

'The hell I am.' Miller swallowed back the tightness rising in his throat. 'You started it — smoke must've got into your clothes!' He swallowed again. 'Oh, my God . . . Thatcher — in there?'

Slamming down the bottle, Beaudine got quickly out of the chair. 'All right. He's dead. There was no other way to get what we needed. He had the — '

'Hold it!' Miller shouted. 'I don't want to hear no more. I want no part of this.'

'You want no — ' Glaring at the deputy Beaudine ditched the rest. 'You're already part of it, Dix. Let us make no mistake about that.'

Miller's head was shaking long before Beaudine was through. 'No — I made a mistake — stood back when Lomax strung up that poor devil. But I've had it. Things are running out of control — there's already been too many

217

killings. I want out.'

Beaudine's laugh cut viciously at him. 'Simply plan to walk away and forget everything, that it?'

'No, not just like that.' Miller pulled himself up to his full height, hooking his thumbs behind his gunbelt. 'I'm going to see Dunn — make a clean breast of everything.'

'That,' Beaudine said very softly, 'would be a severe error in judgement.'

'Wrong. The only mistake I made was falling in with your crooked scheme. But so far I never killed nobody, and it's going to stay that way.'

'No? What about Thatcher?'

Miller wasn't sure he'd heard right. 'What about him?'

'How will you explain going to his house with me — shooting him when he went for a gun?'

'You're crazy! I wasn't nowhere near there!'

'Of course you weren't. But who'll believe you, Dix? And when they find

218

Trent's body who'll believe that wasn't also your handiwork.'

Slowly the deputy's hands freed themselves from the belt. 'Trent . . . too?'

Beaudine nodded picked up the letter-opener, looked at it as though he'd never seen it before. 'Unfortunately, the girl is also in there. Arrived at precisely the wrong time.'

'What . . . girl?' The question was a small, hoarse whisper that scraped across Miller's lips.

'Carol McBride.'

It was the worst thing Beaudine could have said. Miller closed the distance between them, filling both fists with Beaudine's coat. 'You insane bastard! You — killed McBride's — ' The rest choked in his throat as the long blade of a silver letter-opener thrust deep and hard up under his breastbone.

★ ★ ★

219

Trent came to coughing, eyes smarting. A hand went to his throbbing head, came away sticky. Smoke was everywhere, thick and suffocating. For several moments he was a child again, in another house, listening to the unhurried talk of the men who torched it. He shook his head, wincing, forcing his mind back to the present, remembering the shot which, an inch closer would have done a lot more than just graze his skull. Around him flames crawled up the papered walls, devouring the printed pattern, licking hungrily across the carpet. He wasn't sure if the muffled voices he heard were real or simply sounds from the past. Without even thinking about the unimportance of it, he reached for his hat which lay beside him, got up, almost stumbling, turned for the door, and stopped, again shaking his head. Another voice . . . softer, nearer. A woman's voice . . . trying to scream, but not able to raise more than choking gasps.

Behind him were noises.

The handle of the door rattled. A male voice shouted, 'Break it in,' and what might have been a body thudded dully against heavy wood. 'Hurry, dammit, Charlie's probably in there!'

Trent tried to block out the sounds, ears straining in the direction from which he'd heard those cries. Ahead was a bright aperture of orange that had recently been a doorway . . . Tears poured from his eyes, blinding him. He dragged the sleeve of his shirt across them, pulled his neckerchief up over his mouth and nose, and continued on.

One look into the room and he knew it was a waste of time. Nothing could survive in that. Inside, an unseen object crashed loudly, sending a shower of sparks and a burst of darker flame up at the ceiling. He tried calling, but the words came out in a dry cough he had to battle to stop.

And then he saw another kind of movement, heard that voice again. Faint, whimpering. Pulling his hat down tight so that the brim afforded some shield for his eyes, he covered the rest of his face with an arm, and went through. Flames reached out like the hands of beggars, trying to delay him.

She was crouched in a corner, a rug or curtain, or some other thing she'd found, wrapped around her shoulders and head. He fought a way across the room, collided with a chair and went sprawling. The girl screamed, louder this time. He got up, and through the smoke saw the body and the thing of smeared brown above its shoulders.

'Get up,' he croaked, reaching where the girl crouched. So far it was the only corner of the room still untouched by fire, but within another few seconds the flames would have swallowed that also. The girl struggled upright. He flung an arm around her shoulders, another under her legs, sweeping her up from the floor.

Back in the hall, fire now flickered across the carpet like a hundred tentacles, reaching at the door, anxious to consume it. 'Hold tight,' he muttered, ignoring everything but that exit against which battered a thing much harder than a human shoulder.

The handle was hot under his hand. He turned it, but it did nothing. Whoever had closed the door had used a key to lock it from the outside.

The girl must have realized what had happened. In his arms she twisted slightly. 'Above the frame — ' And whatever else was intended got lost in a spasm of coughing that racked her entire body. Trent put her back on her feet, ran a hand quickly along the top of the frame, and found a key. A moment later he was pushing the girl through the open door, out into the cool night air.

There were a whole mob of them around the burning house, given up on trying to douse it with water, watching the flames gorge away at it. They'd moved the sorrel further down the street, taken Carol to O'Conner's surgery. Someone brought Trent a bucket of water which he used to slosh over his head and arms, wondering how he'd been so lucky as to get out of there with no more than a few minor burns and a slight scorching.

He was rolling down his sleeves when three riders forced a way through the gawking spectators. Leading them was Virgil Dunn.

'Was told I'd find you here,' he said. 'You up to riding?'

Trent nodded, fitted his hat to his aching head. He didn't have to ask if anything was wrong; Dunn's face had already revealed that.

'Myrna McBride just rode in,' Dunn said. 'Says Lomax defied her orders and took the crew for a hell ride on Triangle.'

Trent swore quietly, but loud enough for anyone close to hear. 'Where's Miller?'

'Damned if I know. Can't find him, and I ain't waiting.'

★　★　★

In the darkened bunkhouse Lafe and Shorty took stock of their situation. 'Better start prayin' for a miracle, or that those critters get tired and go home,' Shorty said. 'I got a lousy eight rounds left.'

'Only five on this side,' said Lafe, going back to keeping watch from his window. Both had discarded the carbines and were clutching sixguns. 'Wonder why they're suddenly so damn quiet? Must be all of a quarter-hour since last we heard from them.'

Hardly had he spoken when from directly across the yard the guns opened up again, lead slamming into wood, ripping through the windows like a swarm of infuriated hornets, preventing the cornered pair from offering any return fire, even if they'd had the spare gun power to do so.

'Going home,' observed Lafe, 'is obviously not one of the things on their minds.' He looked about the room, not able to see much. 'Hope I'm wrong, but I got a bad feeling about what's up their sleeves.'

'Gonna smoke us out? That what you're thinkin'?'

'They get a couple of men behind us they could have the place burning in no time flat. Either that or — ' Lafe was still turning toward the door when it crashed open. Two men stood for a moment silhouetted against the opening. They dropped what looked like a pole from one of the corrals, leaping swiftly away from the battered door. A third who'd been stationed at their rear shoved forward, thunder hammering from both hands.

Shorty heard his partner grunt, swung about and sent two fast shots through the opening. The figure standing there seemed to lift up high on his heels before vanishing from sight. The men concealed on the outside looked at where Ben Keller had fallen, exchanged quick glances, and started backing away.

'You all right?' Shorty asked, looking over his shoulder, into the shadows.

226

'Fine,' Lafe muttered, and Shorty knew he lied.

'You hurt,' he hollered, 'say so.'

'Don't fret,' Lafe growled, fumbling around, trying to find his gun. 'I'm not going to die on you.'

Shorty was about to say something when a new barrage of fire opened up, only this time it didn't appear to be directed at them. Hoofs were once more pounding the hard-packed earth, as gunfire echoed from all around. He rushed back to the window.

'I'll be damned,' he said. 'Can't see who the hell they are, but looks like the cavalry may just have rode in.'

Trent, Dunn and the two men he'd recruited came into the yard at a fast gallop, firing low at anything that moved outside of the house. Someone ran clear of the shadow of the bunkhouse, tried to get lost in the dark pool under the cottonwoods, and was stopped in his tracks by one of Dunn's deputies.

Their fire was returned, but the

227

manner in which the newcomers circled and criss-crossed the open, like rampaging Apaches, a lot of lead went wasted.

'Put down your guns!' Dunn yelled. 'My name's Dunn — Town Marshal at Twilight — and this's the last time I tell you! One more shot, and s'help me, you'll curse your mothers for bearing you!'

One brave heart fired twice at where the marshal sat his horse. Dunn and Trent returned the compliment almost as one, and then came silence.

'Ten seconds,' Dunn shouted. 'After that, no more talking. Next time you travel, it'll be wrapped in your slickers.'

'Hold your fire,' a voice called. 'I'm comin' out.'

First one, then moments afterwards, another appeared, hands reaching for stars. Dunn yelled one more time and a third man showed himself.

'So're we.' The call came from the bunkhouse, and Shorty stepped out, grinning widely. 'Always said I was too

y

228

good-looking to make an early corpse.'

Lafe emerged clutching at a blood-soaked shoulder, looked at where the three Diamond M hands stood.

'What happened to Lomax?' he frowned.

16

Trent knew he might only be guessing about where Lomax had disappeared to, but he knew he wasn't wrong about that hazy figure who'd shot at him in Thatcher's burning house.

It had already been pushed hard that night, but as if sensing the urgency that possessed its rider, the sorrel made the miles vanish fast under its pounding hoofs.

Smoke still hovered over the town, a scarlet glow reflected off a small bank of low drifting clouds, but he gave it no more than a quick glance, allowing the horse to find its own pace when entering the incline rolling down toward the clustered buildings.

As they neared the start of the wide, deserted street, he brought the animal to a walk, right hand lax at his side, eyes flitting to every doorway, cautious of any slight movement.

They passed Jean's shop, dark now, and he experienced a quick recall of their last meeting. It seemed like a very long time ago, not this very same night.

In his office, Hugh Beaudine frantically stuffed papers into the leather case, angered to find his hands shaking, heart thumping against his ribs. Gladly would he have killed the man who stood waiting and watching.

'Hurry it up,' Lomax said. 'There's no telling how soon they'll find me gone.'

'All right.' Beaudine slammed shut a desk drawer. 'But there are documents I can't afford to leave behind.' Soon — very soon — he was going to have to get rid of Evan Lomax.

'Imagine Miller must've been plenty surprised, dying the way he did.' Lomax managed a thin humorless smile. 'That's a big one, Beaudine. You kill a lawman, even a punk kid like Miller, it gets around in one hell of a hurry.'

Beaudine closed the case, snapped

the catches. 'It won't, if you keep your mouth shut.'

'Sure,' Lomax sneered, 'after helping you dump him in back of that alley, I'm going to shout it out in every saloon.' He moved to the door. 'Ready?'

Beaudine nodded and came out from behind the desk.

'One thing we better take care of now,' Lomax said. 'I need travelling money.'

Cursing in his throat, Beaudine put down the case, reached under his coat, stopping sharply when Lomax's hand rose to touch the butt of his gun. Very carefully he produced his wallet and plucked loose several bills.

'That's exactly half of what I've got.'

Without counting it, Lomax stowed the money away in a shirt pocket. 'It'll do for now. But in case we get separated, remember you still owe me big.'

'That the only reason you came back?' Beaudine snarled, hating the man for failing in what he'd set out to do.

'Let's git,' Lomax said, letting the question go on by. He opened the door, starting down the wooden steps to the street. Still mulling over his immediate position, Beaudine followed.

Though they may never get Triangle, nothing was entirely lost. Not as far as he was personally concerned. He had the papers to all the other properties, endorsed in his favor. If the New York bunch weren't interested he could find others who were. He could sell, pay back the money he'd been advanced, and still retain a very handsome profit. Trent and Thatcher were both dead, no longer able to speak of what they knew. There was really nothing to criminally implicate him. Thatcher, he could claim, had been his agent. Everything had been conducted in a perfectly legitimate manner. Unless Lomax's failure had done something that might bring the law around his neck ... In the meantime, there was nothing left for him here, so why take unnecessary risks by waiting to find out?

They were halfway down the steps when Trent showed himself.

'Going someplace?'

Lomax went rigid. So he'd been right. It was Trent he'd seen ride in with Dunn and the others. It had been too dark to see clearly, and he hadn't stuck around to make certain, which was why he'd not even mentioned it to Beaudine. For the longest moment in the universe everything seemed to come to a stop as they stood staring at each other. Then his hand dipped, moving so fast it would have gone unseen in the dimmed light.

Two shots ripped asunder the silence of the street, one following a brief second after the other. The narrow skull-face broke into a grin as Lomax looked down the steps. It was all wrong; it was never supposed to end this way. The gun he held began to grow excessively heavy, started to drag his arm down, wrenching the smile from his face. As well, he thought, he'd never told Trent about Ezee Strachan. That would have been giving him too much.

A wide-eyed Hugh Beaudine gaped at Lomax paused before him, saw a leg begin to buckle, then watched as his body pitched headlong down the steps.

He wanted to scream something at Trent — anything that would make him lower the gun. But the words stuck like sawdust in his throat. He didn't know when he'd dropped the case, nor how his own gun had appeared in his shaking hand, but suddenly he was firing. Twice he squeezed the trigger before a fist of iron slammed into his shoulder and knocked him hard against the closed door to his office.

Trent came slowly up the steps, the Colt leading the way.

'Don't shoot . . . ' Beaudine cast aside the nickel-plated pistol. 'For the love of God — don't kill me . . . '

'Not me,' Trent said quietly. 'Somebody else'll take care of that chore.

First, though, you've got a week's talking to do.'

★　★　★

Early the next morning the fat owner of the hotel brought Trent a message: Myrna McBride wished to see him in her room. He shaved and dressed, then went to call on her.

It was a different person who invited him to sit down, no longer the proud woman he'd met on two previous occasions.

She said, 'I don't know how to say this; it's most difficult. I owe you something, not merely for saving Carol's life, but for — '

Trent got out of the chair. 'You don't owe me a dime.'

'Please,' she said, also rising, 'don't go — not without hearing me out.' Her hands wrestled each other. She walked to the window, looked out, then turned back to face him. 'I've been a foolish woman. I let Hugh Beaudine convince me of the intelligence of annexing those other ranches, and' — her voice became very soft — 'I helped him persuade Rory likewise . . . allowed him to hire scum like Lomax and Alton.'

'And so some good men died,' Trent said. 'You're going to have to live with that, Mrs McBride. There isn't a thing I can do to make it any easier.' He thought of what Beaudine had revealed about Charlie Thatcher, wondering if she'd been told. But he wasn't going to ask. If she didn't know, she would, soon enough. He moved to the door, wanting to be away from her, but with his hand on the knob, he held back.

'Might've been a good set-up had Baker and your daughter married. Pity you couldn't have seen it that way. But that's over, and all you can do now is pick up the pieces and carry on. There isn't any other way. A lot of work's going to be needed at the Diamond. At Triangle also. But there are a couple of men there, good men, who might even still want to help you.

237

Don't pass them by.'

He opened the door.

'Mr Trent — I — I'm sorry.'

'Yeah — well, that helps some, I guess. Now if you'll excuse me, I've a funeral to attend.'

* * *

Later, he found Shorty and Lafe leaned up against the bar in The Avalon, bought a round of drinks and said his farewells. Outside, his warbags were packed and straddling the sorrel. He swung into the saddle, turned from the hitchrack and walked the horse down the street.

Jean Arden was standing on the edge of the boardwalk in front of her store, waiting. He stopped, got down, and went to her.

'You're leaving . . . ' she said.

'Everything's done and I'm long past getting home.' He shifted his feet uneasily. 'Said I wouldn't go without saying goodbye.'

A familiar mist floated up behind the blue of her eyes. 'Then this . . . is goodbye?'

'Wouldn't work, Jean. Once before you walked out on me, right before we were to be married.'

'Will . . . I explained . . . ' The mist was turning to moisture, threatening to flood her eyes. 'It was the uncertainty of your job — never knowing if you'd live through the day, if I'd be brought news that you — ' The rest broke off in a small sob. 'But I was wrong . . . I made a mistake. I loved you — I never stopped.'

'But you married Hammond, remember?'

Jean Arden stiffened, bowed her head. 'I made a a lot of mistakes.'

He said, 'Goodbye, Jean,' turned and climbed into leather.

At the end of the street, he stopped, twisted around to take one last look at the town called Twilight. Jean stood where he'd left her. He brought the horse around, rode slowly back the way he'd come. When he reached her, he said, 'Guess everybody's entitled to a mistake or two. Right?'

THE END